IT IS TO LAUGH

Collected Short, Humorous and

Twisted Writings.

David Ammons

ISBN: 979-8-7204-6477-6

BURBANK YACHT CLUB

The Burbank Yacht Club is a lighthearted figment of my imagination that came about as the result of joining a yacht club in Marina del Rey, coupled with my appreciation of the absurd. So with just a little exaggeration, you could get a sense of the ridiculous stratification of bureaucracy, and sense of entitlement, combined with a fun atmosphere. Not to mention our club motto, stolen from Wee Robbie Burns, 'Gang Aft Agley.' It comes from his poem, 'To a Mouse,'which is a play on the proverb,'the best laid plans of mice and men, gang aft agley.' Often go astray, in the Scottish vernacular. Another touch is the wrong way compass rose which serves as the club logo. All of which is to say, whatever can go wrong, will.

The genesis of the club was with an old friend of mine who had started a 'fire company' organized around an old fire engine he had restored. He invented a membership with fanciful titles, etc., which made me think of the BYC. The joke being that Burbank is a landlocked community. I started with a poster featuring the club's first 'Flagship' the Arroyo Seco (dry river bed), on a parched desert. The poster stated membership was open and that meetings would be held weekly at this location. Another friend of mine who owns a restaurant directly across the street from Warner Bros. Studio in Burbank, insisted the poster be hung in his restaurant, and the legend was born.

The only thing left to do was publish a logbook of typical club activities chronicling the events of the club. These I present here in hopes that you can enjoy a chuckle at the absurdity of those, fictional, events. I present myself as Commodore, pro tem, only because the pro tem part is meant to show the temporary nature of life, in general, and to show that whoever wants this job can have it. So here goes...

A TIME TO FORGIVE

As a part of the (non monetary) "settlement" we are working through from last year's Easter, uh, festivities, I (as your Commodore) was required to apologize to the membership, local emergency officials, the marina management and staff, and for the sake of brevity: etc., etc. Given the number of people involved and to provide some dignity to the affair, the board decided to have this take place in the club's Grand Ballroom as part of the announcement of THIS year's holiday events.

I must say, I looked pretty dapper marching to the podium, dressed in my starched "whites" slapping my walking crop in my palm to the beat of the club's anthem, as played by our cadet marching band. I noticed a number of our Ladies Auxiliary group squirming in their seats at my display of the crop. Not certain what that is all about, but rest assured I will get to the bottom of it.

But I digress.

Having had time to reflect on last year's unfortunate turn of events, it might be easy for one to say we should have been able to foresee the potential problems. I disagree, but will let the reader decide. Where to begin? Well, one would have to begin with the idea that the club, trying to make the event non religious, decided to make it a fun day for the kiddos. One of the members, recalling an activity from his youth, suggested an egg hunt, with a twist.

We would make it, instead, a dyed-peep hunt. One need only imagine the colorful pageantry of such an event unfolding on the club's generous grounds to see why we voted to go with this suggestion.

In hindsight it might have been better to go straight religion on the day. But, that too, was ruined a few years ago when we had to allow someone, in PC fairness and in a spirit of ecumenical fervor, set up a velvet covered altar in the basement, replete with restraints and surrounded by Tiki Torches borrowed from the pool area. That ended badly, as well, when a number of our male members complained of wives going missing for hours, during some of our "drinkfest" parties. Well, you just can't please everyone.

But, again, I digress.

Having no idea where, or how, to get our
hands on several hundred live chicks, let
alone dyed, one of the board members
recalled hearing that our dock boy, Daboo
had some experience in this area. We
called Daboo-the-dock-boy into the
meeting. Traditions die hard in Yacht club
circles, dock "boy" is a title of distinction,
even though Daboo had to be nearing 60 by
this time. And, though he had been with
the club most of his adult life, this was the
first I could ever recall him being actually
IN the main clubhouse. Anyway, Daboo
claimed that he had, indeed been a chicken
herder in his native country, a
small principality on the Silk Road, near
the Honyockastani border. We had found
our man!

On the big day the weather was glorious, as
the little tykes, all dressed in their finest

nautical toggery waited anxiously as Daboo prepared to release the chicks. The idea being to allow them a one minute head start before releasing the kiddos to hunt them down and claim their brightly colored prizes. A flare gun was fired and the chicks were released. The count down had barely begun for the kids to begin the hunt when all eyes went skyward to the rows of tall trees lining the quarter mile entrance drive into the club. Apparently the colorful display below had attracted the hawks which inhabit the treetops of the club. They began to swoop in time and time again hitting and taking chick after chick in an explosion of pastel pinfeathers (mesmerizing in a way) the kiddies shouting and crying as their parents ran to them trying to shield their eyes from the carnage taking place. The commotion also attracted a pack of coyotes which live in the far reaches of the arroyo. They began working the fringes of the herd, picking off a few that were missed, or merely maimed, by the hawks. It was right about then that things really got off the rails. Some of our members, many of whom are former military, got the idea of scaring off the wildlife by firing our huge ceremonial cannon into the air, which they did. And it worked. The sly coyotes bolted back into the confines of the arroyo. The only problem being that the cannoneers forgot to check the barrel before firing it off. Evidently, a few of our underage cadet corps had been snitching beers and hiding the empties in the cannon. Needless to say this set up a scene reminiscent of the ack-ack during the Battle-of-Britain. The hawks began falling out of the sky like so many Junkers JU 88 bombers.

That really panicked the crowd and they all ran toward the docks, along with the remaining chicks, startled by the blast. The crowd got to witness the last of the chicks jumping off the seawalls and being taken by a school of Barracuda which tend to hang there in the spring. Not sure why the chicks jumped, as far as I know, even adult chickens are not strong swimmers. I guess, as an old sailing buddy of mine once put it. It's hard to think strategically when your ass is on fire.

Needless to say, Daboo is no longer with the club, this being his third offense, counting the altar in the basement brouhaha. For all of this I deeply apologize.

I remain your,

Commodore, pro tem
Burbank Yacht Club
"Gang Aft Agley"

A GLORIUS FOURTH...

Well, with the embarrassing, but minor, fiasco of the Easter event behind us we figured that the big 4th of July Decorated Dinghy Parade would provide some long overdue respite for the club and its members. It is the sad duty of your Commodore, pro tem, to report that this was not the case. The only bright spot is that this time, at least, I was not the focal point of the issue.

It was that damned Darlene Shaminski and her Daisy Duke's, replete with American flag bikini top.

Everything would have been fine if her husband, "Doobie", had just been his normal laid back self. But, no. The Doobmeister had to choose this weekend to go cold turkey with the wacky tobacky.

Anyway, things started off beautifully on the manicured (some say marinated) grounds of the club, with the ceremonial firing of the club cannon, after a check down the barrel for any, ahem, detritus (See Easter posting). And, as per usual, everyone was dressed casually for the hi-jinks filled, and waterlogged event. Given the proximity to water, access to booze, and thirty-five, or so, small overpowered inflatables, what could go wrong?

The firing of the cannon signals the "dash to the dinghies" which are lined up along the club pier, all draped in bunting for the occasion. The idea is to parade the creatively and patriotically decorated dinghies around the marina with throngs of cheering folks basically throwing beer bottles, beach chairs, and otherwise trying to scuttle the Lilliputian armada by firing Roman Candles at enfilade. Were that the redcoats had been that accurate. (Reminder: note to marina board of governors regarding rowdy crowd behavior).

Leading the procession in the club's official dinghy, the One Ringhy Dinghy, I try to present myself as Washington crossing the Delaware, dressed in period costume, with one booted foot on the bow trying to affect a countenance of glorious and hopeful anticipation, as I duck Roman Candle volleys (powdered wigs are extremely flammable).

And that's when it all started. This woman in the crowd lining the docks took umbrage (gotta love that word) with Darlene using the flag to cover her, um, parts. Well, Darlene, who had been hitting the bottomless Harvey Flagbangers (chilled vodka with strawberries and blueberries) pretty heavily at the pre-parade bruncheon was having none of that from some mousey blonde who was using red Chuck Taylor's to complete her holiday tri-color theme.

"At least I have something to cover," Darlene shouted back, and therewith popped the string and let those babies fly. That's when the parade ended.

The rest of the flotilla began circling the Shaminski dinghy like someone had thrown a picnic ham in the middle of a pod of killer whales. Doobie, suddenly galvanized by his new sobriety, leapt to defend his wife's, er, honor (I mean it's not like none of the men in the club had ever seen her..uh, another story, another time). In his zeal to cover her with random decorations while she was twerking, or doing some strange version of the Pony on the bow of the dinghy, he inadvertently kicked the helm over and maxed out the throttle. This threw him to the deck of the dinghy with a flag wrapped around his head.

The dinghy shot into the shipping lanes and a bow line got entangled in the lines of a passing cargo container ship, the Sushi Maru. It looked like Darlene had gone into her "party trance" (more on that in another post) and appeared to have shifted into the bugaloo.

As the sun began to set, the Sushi Maru, according to the Shipfinder app, was headed to Yokohama at 18 knots with a gaggle of dinghies in pursuit, but losing headway steadily.

Another mess to be dealt with....

As always, your,

Commodore, pro tem
Burbank Yacht Club
"Gang Aft Agley"

LABOR OF LOVE, DAY WEEKEND

Well, another Labor Day weekend has come and gone here at the BYC.

But the debris field remains...
Yes, what started out as a foolproof plan for innocent fun, once again, managed to wash up on your Commodore's beach in a disastrous way. I ask you, what could go wrong with an event like, "Bold Cars and Old Tars", which featured old-time muscle cars, and a flotilla of antique wooden boats from days of yore? Let me tell you...

We thought it would be fitting to have one of the muscle cars perched atop the recently installed "Floating Island" in the club's inlet area. We got the idea from the PGA golf tour where they install a car in such a way that the car seems to be floating on the surface of the water at different venues on the tour each week.

We even decided to have a "King" and "Queen" for the event. The King was determined to be, appropriately, a 1971, "Boat Tail", Buick Riviera, cherished possession of one of our members, Eddie Lemayne. The Queen, of course, would be our own original flagship, the 45 foot Arroyo Seco. We took her out of mothballs for this special occasion. She was built in the late 60's at the legendary Dufresne boatyards in Zihuatanejo, and was a great example of the golden age of wooden yachts.

Anyway, we thought it would be a good idea to have our Rear Admiral, "Doobie" Shaminsky give the boat a mini-shakedown cruise prior to the event since it had been a while since anyone had her out. Well, his "doob-ness" decided about 2 hours into the shakedown that it might be a good idea to have a few hits on a Fatboy, which he had brought along. But he only had one match. He rightly reckoned that it would be better to have a renewable source of flame for his Fatboy. He wrongly reckoned that source to be the original equipment alcohol fuel stove.

In the meantime, on a beach near Malibu, a "D List" celebrity wedding was taking place. Local cook-show hostess, Mindy Macher was getting hitched to channel 99's weekend weather wonk, Lex Lopress. It being the 3rd for her and his 4th, they had arranged to have a flower boat set aflame and sent out to sea in a Viking burial ceremony representing their past lovers and spouses. It was a rather large craft. At the appropriate cue, the boat was set aflame

and sent to sea on the tide giving off a
scent of tropical flowers.

Just as the flaming mass was hissing its last
and sinking, the horizon was filled with
another flaming craft, sailing hell bent for
leather toward the beach giving off a scent
of Asian hash. To the consternation of the
wedding planners and to the delight of the
guests, they watched as the craft was
consumed by flames just as it hit the beach
and disgorged a black-faced Doobie with a
loud splash.
Mindy was leading the crowd rushing to
help the survivor. As she reached him and
cradled his head in her arms witnesses say
she exclaimed, "Doobie?" To which
Doobie replied, "Mindy?" Turns out
Doobie had been Mindy's number two.
Meanwhile, back at the club, everyone was
admiring the levitating act of the Buick on
the water, right up to the point of the tide
coming in. And a flood tide at that.

Apparently, golf ponds do not have tidal swings. Fortunately for Eddie Lemayne, the Harbor Patrol changed the citation from operating a craft without a permit, as the old Buick tried valiantly to stay afloat, to creating a hazard to navigation, after it sank. A slightly lesser fine.

No one has seen the Arroyo Seco, Doobie or Mindy since. So far, I have been able to duck the calls of Lex Lopress, Mrs. Shaminsky, Eddie LeMayne, and the insurance company. I remain your -

Commodore, pro tem
Burbank Yacht Club
"Gang Aft Agley"

THE PUMPKIN'S RED GLARE

You would think the Burbank Yacht Club, one of the largest and most prestigious yacht clubs on the west coast, could pull off a simple Halloween party without a hitch. Wouldn't you? It is my sad duty to report, that was not the case. So, once again, your old Commodore, pro tem, is left to clean up the mess.

The board appointed our Vice Rear Admiral of the Exchequer, Richard Weed, to head up this year's festivities. In retrospect, a poor choice since being the treasurer of the club, he decided to save some money by having the party in the boathouse annex. The annex is a little-used facility located away from the main buildings. Its first level is used primarily for long-term boat storage. The second level is an old hall which Richard figured had built-in creepiness, what with the cobwebs, dust and all.

The first order of business was to pick a theme. We ended up with, "Buoys and Ghouls". In order to publicize the event, we placed a number of small pumpkins in the sling of one of the club's boat-lift cranes. In the sling dangling under the armature of the other crane, we hoisted the largest pumpkin grown in the county this year. Between the two slings, we attached a banner proclaiming the upcoming event.

It was decided that 100 jack-o-lanterns be carved and illuminated by candles, the flickering of which providing a nice eerie touch. Then the committee opted to dress the hall in streamers and garlands of black and orange crepe paper. A material later referred to by the Fire Marshal as the "accelerant".

Yep, you guessed it. The dancing got a little crazy, thanks to everyone being jacked up on pumpkin spice martinis. Then someone knocked a tableful of jack-o-lanterns over and that was all she wrote. In their haste to get out of the burning building, one of the celebrants tripped the spring-loaded crane holding the small pumpkins. The suddenly released armature flung the pumpkins into the channel like a load of grapeshot from a cannon. Unfortunately, most of them landed on the deck of the 70' Scheherazade, the flagship of a rival club. It was all pimped out as a pirate ship for their themed Halloween party, the "Aaaargonauts Ball." Apparently, between the booze and the natural rivalry, they thought the attack was intentional. They rolled their ceremonial cannon out and loaded it with candy corn and began to repeatedly pepper the fleeing BYC members.

Well, sir, our Sergeant at Arms, Stewart Gotz, was having none of that and he released the latch on the second spring-loaded crane with the giant prize winner in its sling. As the glorious gourd arched over the flaming annex with tatters of the banner streaming proudly behind, I couldn't help but think of Fort Sumpter and the inspiration for our national anthem. If only for a moment. The sickening ka-thump of a 600-pound pumpkin striking the Scheherazade square amidships brought me back to reality.

Even today, as I stand amid the ashes of the annex and survey the channel, blocked with the wreckage of our rival's flagship, a small quiver of pride runs down my spine.

And Thus I remain,

Commodore, pro tem
Burbank Yacht Club
"Gang Aft Agley"
DAMN THE TORPEDOS...

Feeding the less fortunate on Thanksgiving Day. What could be a nobler task, I ask you? It promised to be such a wonderful gesture of kindness and generosity on the part of the club. Ah yes, promises. Where did it all go wrong?

To begin with, as part of the day's activities, we decided to have a "reenactment" of the Mayflower landing at Plymouth Rock. We further decided that our current flagship, Arroyo Seco III, being the largest sailing vessel in our fleet, should play the part of the Mayflower. And what would a landing be without a band of "pilgrims"? Oh, and throw in a hastily expropriated boulder as the "Rock". Hard to believe what took weeks in the planning (two weeks, alone, to run down boat shoes with buckles) could so quickly unravel.

Playing not an insignificant role in that unraveling was the committee's decision to have char-broiled turkey served by a local catering group known as "El Poco Pollo". They even provided a big charcoal broiling cooker on wheels, which was placed at the head of our main dock. Looking down from the Grand Promenade of the club, it presented a beautiful and bountiful picture. Even if the mariachi music playing over the P.A., which the caterers insisted upon, was a little incongruous for the occasion.

It was decided, in a final blow to sanity, to have a ceremonial turkey sacrificed at the altar of the Rock which had been placed on the dock at the landing spot of the "Mayflower". You may recall from an earlier post, Daboo-the-dock-boy, who we

dismissed after a number of, er, in-
discretionary events at the club, was raised
as a chicken herder in his native
Honyockistan. So, against our better
judgment, and under the shadow of a letter
threatening an illegal dismissal suit from
the Honyockistani Embassy, we decided to
rehire Daboo. Besides which, with his
training among the fowl of his country, he
was rumored to be a legendary turkey
whisperer.

And, so it was on that fateful day, the
"Mayflower" pulled off a perfectly
executed landing and tied up at the Rock,
to the applause of the assemblage of less
fortunates. Who knew they had an
appreciation of sailing skills? Anyway,
Daboo, represented the Wampanoag savior,
Squanto, but was decked out more like
a Central Casting version of Cochise
replete with warpaint. All were amazed as
Daboo, whispering incantations, led a

perfectly behaved 30 pound Tom turkey down the gangplank to his fate at the Rock. Committee chair, Assistant Vice Rear Admiral Eddy Lemayne, holding the axe, the dropping of which would signal the beginning of dinner, acknowledged those gathered to partake. The would-be diners lined the upper dock area holding plates and utensils, leading to the huge torpedo shaped broiler.

Living up to his reputation, Daboo rubbing his fingers under the gullet of the turkey and giving a final incantation of some magic words, laid the giant bird's neck across the rock. Lo, and behold, with a final gobble, the bird stayed in position as Daboo, like a magician levitating an audience volunteer, his arms and head upraised chanted some weird gibberish in his native tongue. Then the axe fell...

Well, sir, I've never seen such a ruckus and hope to never again. The now headless turkey jumped a good ten feet in the air, wings flapping, feathers flying, and made a beeline straight up the gangplank toward the the upper dock. Those in line to eat, wanting no part of this, fled the scene throwing dinner plates, cups and napkins skyward in their panicked retreat. Unfortunately, one of them accidentally dislodged a block wedged under the wheels of the broiler, sending it down the gangplank toward the Rock and the "Mayflower". Helpless to stop the white-hot broiler, Daboo and Eddy Lemayne jumped off the dock into the slip basin. As they bobbed to the surface they, like the survivors of the Battle of Midway, watched in horror as the torpedo, picking up steam, blasted into the rock, propelling its coals onto the deck of the club's flagship. That, in turn, caused the "pilgrims" to jump-ship, post haste, as the resultant flames spread too quickly to be extinguished. All to the strains of, an uptempo, Mexican Hat Dance.

Later, in my offices high atop the club, and with the last wisps of smoke from the remains of the A.S. III wafting past my balcony, I met with Daboo and Eddy. My Steward, Jingo, had placed some plastic drop cloths on my brocade furniture and carpet to protect it from the dripping, and chagrined, pair. I asked Daboo why, this time, he shouldn't be banished permanently from the club. 'Turkey whisperer, indeed', I snorted.
In his sopping defense, and in his heavily accented English, he stated, "Ven za turkey has no head, zare are no ears to hear za vispers."

I had to admit, the bedraggled little warrior made a good point....

I remain your,
Commodore, pro tem
Burbank Yacht Club
"Gang Aft Agley"

BOAT PARADE BLUES

Well, I should have known things were not going to go well at this year's Christmas Boat Parade when Jingo my manservant and personal steward was fitting me with a Santa suit for the festivities to come that evening. Oh, I know you think the life of a club Commodore living in a penthouse suite high atop the club is one of glamor and glitz, but let tell you it is not. While being fitted for my annual appearance as Santa, Jingo had the audacity to mention that I probably wouldn't need as much padding this year to play jolly old Saint Nick. So it is not all gooseberry tea and sugarplum scones here at the top. Well maybe part of it is but the rest really is padding.

Did I mention how hard it is to get volunteers to work on the decoration committee? To the point that I continue to have to rely on the usual suspects year in and year out. That should have been my second tipoff right there. Due to the lack of anyone else stepping-up, I had to appoint Eddie LeMayne Who was already on double probation for past screw-ups, as this year's boat decorating chairman. And, of course, when you select Eddie it comes as automatic that you get his sidekick 'Doobie' Shaminsky as a throw-in. Sort of like a 1 and 1A entry in a $600 claiming stakes race. And of course with 'Doobie' you get his wife Darlene. Yes, she took him back after the beach wedding fiasco (see commodore's log entry from 9/23/15 "Labor of love...")

Anyway, as you know I am a hands-off supervisor, I like to let the committees work their magic and just keep me abreast of their progress from time to time (you'd think I'd learn). So, this year's theme was 'Hands Across the Water.' As I leaned on the observation deck of my suite one bright morning last week, I saw to my dismay that Eddie had taken the theme in a literal direction. A giant hand had been constructed on the Arroyo Seco IV laced with 200,000 twinkling lights.

I immediately had Eddie come to my office for a full report of the goings-on. he arrived with another of his conscripts, Daboo the Dock-boy. Now some say that Daboo predated the club when he began working the docks upon arrival from his native Honyockistan some 50 years previous. 'The Dock-boy' just sort of stuck as part of his name, over the years. He had just in the past year been granted 'house' privileges and allowed to enter the halls of the club despite a few previous, ahem, transgressions. Part of the reason he tagged along with Eddie was to show off his elf outfit, complete with a long beard which I questioned. The little rascal told me it was a tradition in his native land that elves had beards.

No matter, I had other things to deal with, including the big hand. Eddie explained that it was animatronic and would actually wave to the crowd and judges as we passed the reviewing stand and, at the same time, open the doors of a small sentry post surrounded by toy soldiers to reveal me, cuckoo-clock-like, dressed in Santa's finest. Somewhat reassured I let them continue. Eddie could be very persuasive when he wanted to be. However, I should have asked about the roles to be played by Doobie and Darlene. As they say, hindsight is always 20/20.

So on the night of the big boat parade there we were, all set to go with the Doobmeister at the helm and Darlene looking very fetching in a skimpy 'Mrs. Claus' outfit which featured a red halter top with flashing lights synchronized with the rest of the display lights. According to Eddie.

I wasn't totally shocked to find out later that his Doobness had gotten into some Acapulco Gold just prior to shoving off. Or, that Daboo in a Clark Griswold moment was to stand atop the sentry hut and lip-synch 'Joy to the World' and plug in the cords that would light and set in motion the giant waving hand, Darlene's halter top, and open the doors of the Guard hut simultaneously. Unfortunately, it also set in motion the end of the Arroyo Seco IV.

Yes, my fellow members, it is my sad duty to report that Doobie decided to throw a little jink in the course just as the Arroyo Seco IV was approaching the Judges Stand, causing Daboo to catch a good portion of his beard in the connecting of the cords, resulting in a short circuit. Evidently, it was spectacular to see when, like a lightning bolt, the charge blew off Darlene's top, the crowd thinking it was part of the show erupted in cheers which abruptly died as the bolt jumped to the giant hand causing it to begin gesticulating against the mast and shoot sparks out the top. They say mothers had to avert their children's eyes. I say evidently because the doors to the sentry shack never did open and I was trapped inside a burning box until Doobie, in a moment of lucidity body-blocked it into the main channel, putting out the flames but setting up a Houdini-esque escape on my part to save myself from drowning!

As I sit here now writing this log entry and dreaming of lost glory I am filled with pride that we have once again, at least, captured the coveted Best Pyrotechnic Display burgee.

I remain,

Commodore, pro tem
Burbank Yacht Club
'Gang Aft Agley'

2015 GONE IN A TWINKLING

As I sit in my office, atop the The Burbank Yacht Club, gazing out at the manicured expanse of the club's grounds and reflect upon the past year, my thoughts turn to the club's New Year's Eve Party. Thoughts which, I dare say, are still fresh in my mind.

We, the Committee, decided to have the party "off campus" this year and we selected a beautiful venue in a classic old European style hotel. The Grand Burbank Squalide. Part of the reason for selecting this hotel was they agreed to hire, in a three-party arrangement between the Club, the hotel and the court system, the newly unemployed (see my previous post) Daboo-the-dock-boy. We felt it to be a win-win-win in that the hotel gained a doorman, we got off the hook with the Honyockistani Embassy's court order, and Daboo gained the dignity, as Daboo-the-doorman, of having his title upgraded from boy to man. No raise.

As we entered the hotel for the big event, It was great to see Daboo greeting us and looking very dashing in his garish waistcoat, plumage and pillbox hat, even if he looked, rather disturbingly, like the Captain of the flying monkeys from the Wizard of Oz. Ah, but once in the hotel, our thoughts turned to New Year's merriment promised by the hotel. Its Grand Lobby, which went up 7 floors, and was surrounded by balconies at each level was breathtakingly decorated with sparkling strands of twinkling white lights strung across the balconies at each floor. If you looked straight up for too long, it was an almost migraine inducing vision.

We were further amazed at the decorations adorning the Penthouse Ballroom itself. There in the center was a huge, and finely detailed, ice sculpture depicting our beloved Arroyo Seco IV, the club's former flagship. It brought a tear to my eye as I looked at the ship which proudly displayed, in a tiny ice depiction, the prize burgee for "Best Pyrotechnics". A prize from the Christmas Boat Parade in which she was lost. Truly, she went out in a blaze of glory. Ah, well, a story for another time.

At midnight the tribute band, "The Captain and Camille", began playing Auld Lang Syne, at which point Doobie Shaminsky as Father Time, and his wife Darlene, as the baby new year, were to come out and circle the massive ice sculpture waving to the crowd. The twist was that they were going to do it while the doob-meister, Representing the "old", was going to be riding a skateboard and Darlene would be riding a "new" hoverboard on loan from Daboo, to whom it belonged.

His doobness having spent most of his teen, and for that matter adult, life riding a skateboard had no trouble negotiating the dance floor in a toga, even while carrying a scythe. Darlene, on the other hand was having a little trouble trying to stay astride the hoverboard, balance an oversized hourglass, and keep the 2016 banner covering her, uh, parts. Much to the interest of the men in the crowd.

And so it came to pass that the hoverboard decided to burst into flame. Many of the blotto attendees, thinking it was part of the celebration, began to applaud. It wasn't until the flames leapt to Darlene's banner that they fell into a lush, er, hush. This prompted Doobie to swoop in and snag it off Darlene with his scythe, thereby saving her from disfigurement, if not embarrassment.

In her panic to get off the board, she plowed headlong into the ice sculpture sending it skidding across the floor, out the door, over the railing and into the web of lights below. The twinkling lights and sparks set off by short circuits, floor by floor, reflected off the ice like some insane, mirrored disco ball as the great ship went down. Again. Quite mesmerizing, in its own kaleidoscopic way.

Anyhow, as Jingo, my loyal steward delivers my mid-morning tea dressed in his starched whites, I am heartened by hopes of good tidings for the coming year. Even if, first thing Monday morning I must meet with our attorneys to sort out the mess of Daboo suing us for loss of his hoverboard, our countersuit of him for providing faulty goods, the hotel's suit against us for wrecking the hotel, and Darlene's suit against all of the above for humiliation in extremis, whatever the hell that is...

I remain your,

Commodore, pro tem
Burbank Yacht Club
"Gang Aft Agley"

PLAY ME HEARTS AND FLOWERS

As I sit here in my office high atop our beloved Burbank Yacht Club, looking out at the tree-lined quarter-mile of the entrance road leading up to the circular drive in front of the club. I wonder about our current generation of mariners and worry a bit, as well. Jingo, my loyal steward has just delivered my mid-morning tea using the club's antique silver tea service and cart. Just the way I like it. With a liberal splash of Honey Jack, a twist of lemon and a wee dash of St. Germain. But, alas, as I reflect upon the club motto, "Gang Aft Agley", burnished on each piece of silver, I can't help but wonder whether old Robert Burns had it right. No matter how hard we try, something always manages to go wrong.

My concern regarding the current generation needs some perspective. Our founding membership took part in such historic events as expeditions to the North Pole, discovering new trade routes to China and defeating the Barbary Pirates. One would think with that sort of bloodline, a club could pull off a simple Valentines Day event without a hitch. But, (sigh).

As always, the hiccups begin in the planning process. Whatever possessed the committee to decide that it was a good idea to position Darlene Kaminsky as the bowsprit figurehead of the Arroyo Seco V for the Grand Parade up the "love canal", I have no idea. Although she certainly made a fetching appearance as a bikini topped mermaid. The real lunacy was the idea that Doobie, her husband, would be dangled above her suspended on some jerry-rigged halyard, as Cupid, complete with diaper, bow, and quiver of arrows.

A further issue was the unfortunate choice of name for the event. "Heart of Stone" was certainly a great song from the Stones, and the flower arrangement spelling it out looked terrific running the entire length of the boat. Some of our Cadet Squadron members decided it would be great fun to reconfigure the flower arrangement into something unsuitable for publication here. These hijinks were caught during the rehearsal run which was still going on.

Perhaps I should take some of the blame for not providing better oversight of Committee Chair, Eddie LeMayne, recently busted down to 2nd Assistant Vice Rear Admiral for his chairmanship of the Thanksgiving fiasco.

His chairmanship of the Valentine committee had him being referred to as "Last Chance LeMayne".

At any rate, I'm sitting in my office watching the rehearsal for the arrival of the Love Boat with Darlene practicing her princess wave as Doobie buzzes around above her pretending to shoot arrows at her. Dear God what were they thinking? Meanwhile, our Junior's are circling the big boat in their sabot's and pretending to throw rose petals in the water preceding the boat.

We had ordered several boxes of rose petals from a local florist and several dozen "Valentines" cupcakes from a local bakery and were still awaiting delivery of both. Just then I spied two delivery vans racing up the entrance road, each trying to outdo the other to get their delivery made. They split up at the beginning of the circle, just as Darlene's bikini top became, uh, maladjusted. Well, no need to go into what might go wrong when two distracted drivers traveling at high speed and closing quickly, er, go wrong.

A spectacular head-on collision, spewing the contents of the two vans into the channel in a fantastic explosion of rose petals and Red Velvet cupcakes. The Junior's were bright enough to sail to the docks as Doobie began pulling arrows out of his quiver and shooting them at the red water in some sort of drug-fueled rage. Who knows what he was seeing?

I rang for Jingo and asked him to have former Committee Chair LeMayne step into my office.

I remain your,

Commodore, pro tem
Burbank Yacht Club
 "Gang Aft Agley"

NEVER TRUST A LEPRECHAUN NAMED DABOO

It should have been easy to head this one off, but I must admit I took my eye off the helm due to the re-signing of Daboo-the-dock-boy. Yes, I know, but he looked so forlorn and contrite after having been savagely sacked by the thugs at the Hotel Squalide of Burbank, that I just had to relent. It nearly broke the poor old Honyockistani's spirit to have to grovel at my feet for his old position back. But there was no choice, since the New Year's fiasco in which we traded Daboo to the hotel in return for having our party there.

Anyway, after my personal steward, Jingo, had vacuumed the tears and groveling indentations out of my beautiful oriental carpeting, and Daboo, that little heathen, swore to behave on the head of some God that sounded a lot like Abu Ben Affleck, I took him back. It was good to see the little scamp working the docks again, I must admit.

Which brings me to the opening day calendar bollocks. We usually have our Vice Rear Admiral of the Exchequer, Richard Weed, handle opening day because of the income potential involved. And, sad to say, with all the lawsuits and other expenses mounting, we need every dime. Anyhow, it turns out that Opening Day was scheduled on March, 17th. Yup, St. Paddy's day. A day that Richard had also, as it turns out, booked out the club (as one of the area's largest meeting venues) for an Elect Bernie Sanders event. Don't even start with me about the incongruity of a socialist having an event at a yacht club. Like I said, every dime….

The Opening Day Committee was already at odds with the St Pat's committee over the decorations, and timing of the dual celebrations when the Bernie information hit. This is the kind of, er, stuff that eventually washes up on my beach. The theme for the combined Opening Day, St. Pat's event was to have been, "Hibernian Happening", spelled out in a banner spray of flowers.

In a stroke of leadership befitting Solomon, and not wanting to waste my minor in floral arranging, I move a couple of peonies here, a hyacinth there, and voila, we have, "Hi Bernie, A Happening!" That seemed to appease some of the planners but still left many P.O.'d and bitching about the collapsing of two good drunk days into one, and then wrecking that by having some socialist downer thrown into the mix.

We needn't have worried. Come the day of the event, the membership was working hard from early on, trying to cram two days of drinking into one. The opening ceremonies were to be capped by firing the ceremonial cannon loaded with green confetti to mark the transition to the Sanders event. All neat and tidy with the added inspiration of inviting the Hi Bernians to the big dance following their event - at 60 bucks a pop. A capitalistic twist that had Weed cackling like Snidely Whiplash.

Just as I began to believe we might pull this whole thing off, once again the fates conspired to bring us down. Daboo had been assigned the ceremonial task of loading and firing the cannon, dressed as a leprechaun. His English not being as good as it could be, he made a critical error. When he got the shell from the flare locker, he grabbed a Green Cluster Flare Instead of the Green Confetti Shell.

So, here comes Bernie's double-decker campaign bus down our entrance drive. On the open-air top deck of the bus, a shirt-sleeved and straw-hat-wearing band is playing a spirited version of "Happy Days Are Here Again".

Then, KA-BLAM!!! An earsplitting report of the cannon followed by green flares raking the side of the bus, like a strafing attack on a B-29, sending straw hats, sheet music and instruments flying skyward in a dissonant crescendo.

Thank God no one was injured but the proceeds from the dance, according to Richard Weed, were, um, a little less than anticipated.
I remain your,

Commodore, pro tem
Burbank Yacht Club
"Gang Aft Agley"

TIME TO TAKE THE HELM AGAIN

Okay, it's been a while since you've heard from your leader. Yes, at the urging of many of our members (not to mention the go-bots from FB), it is time for your old Commodore, pro tem, to step back up to the helm. I guess it took a pandemic to flush me out, but anyway, here goes. A number of you called me out as being stupid, if not insane, for suggesting, somewhat tongue in cheek, that we should isolate our elders and those with compromised immune systems, and let the rest of this puppy play out. Well, well, it seems that is the road down which we are headed, with at least three governors calling for just such an action, not that they should be considered judges of sanity or even stupidity, for that matter.

Anyway, following my advice, I am sequestered here in my quarters high above our beloved Burbank Yacht Club and have been for the past three days. Ah, but fear not my friends, I am not alone. In keeping with the old practice of retainer sacrifice, I have quarantined my man-servant Jingo with me, and yes, he shamed me into taking in Daboo the Dock-boy, as well. I guess I'm becoming maudlin in my old age, but after all, Jingo and Daboo are both over 65. And in my case, I may have mentioned in the past, have a touch of Parkinson's.

I am writing this message to let you know that I, in my new circumstance, must relinquish some of my duties to the younger members, loathe as I am to do so. So even though in the past this has not worked out well (see my previous BYC posts), I am begging you to bear with me as I try to guide the Eddie LeMayne's and Doobie Shaminsky's through the coming months. By the way, I saw Doobie yesterday as he skateboarded around the club, poor guy. Darlene, his wife, delivered a bunch of supplies the other day. It was sad, in a way, that she included a note to me asking if she could join us in our sequestration. I felt it my duty to put it to a vote, and her request was voted down 2 to 1. Discretion will not allow me to disclose the breakdown of the majority. However, I can tell you in my lecture of the other two; it came out that Jingo and Daboo had conspired, unbeknownst to me, to order a, ahem, realistic female robot, for them to share. Far be it for me to point out the trouble I can see down the track with THAT idea.

Anyway, friends and members, I am being interrupted in my writing by Jingo as he delivers my mid-morning tea. A delightful blend of tea, honey with a splash of St. Germain, and a dash of Chambord. The perfect elixir to sip from my balcony as I overlook the manicured grounds of our beloved BYC. I hope you will take a moment to look up during your busy days and give me a wave from time to time. In the meantime, I remain -

Commodore, pro tem
Burbank Yacht Club
Gang Aft Agley

Notes for futures...

We had such high hopes for this greenest of days. However, as our club motto, emblazoned beneath our beloved crest, so aptly states, "Gang Aft Agley". For St.

Pats, the board decided we would re-open the long closed, and mostly forgotten, Burbank-to-Toluca Lake Canal which runs along the old, and totally forgotten, rail bed of the Burbank, Delray, Santa Monica line (BDSM). The thought being that we would refill the canal, dye the water green, a la the Chicago River and, at least for the day, float our flagship, the Arroyo Seco lV, upon its emerald waters. Wouldn't you know it, just as the canal became totally full, our crew at attention, and with the cannon blast to begin the lilting strains of McNamara's Band, one of the rotting old lock gates gave way sending the Arroyo Seco lV right down San Fernando Blvd. in a cascade of Irish splendor. God she looked so majestic there…for a moment. We would like to thank the Burbank Business Assn. for incorporating the newly dyed store fronts into the coming weekend's "Blarney Bucks" promotion, and have promised the mall we will have the ship dislodged from the entrance to the parking lot by midnight. (Note to club members: Assessments to follow).

Faith and begorrah, mates,

****

Wow, we just finished the shakedown cruise aboard the Arroyo Seco lV (see previous post). It was so much fun! Our officer in charge of ballast pulled off another masterful job by picking a comfy spot in the cockpit and nary moving a muscle for the entire day at sea except perhaps to swill a little Champagne or try some of the copious snacks provided by Alan, restaurateur and newly minted sommelier (the real deal, just back from Bordeaux). As you may know, this is whale migration season as they head south to winter in the Baja (doesn't everyone?). Alas, in the end, It was another dashing disappointment. We had the grill all fired up and ready to receive some of the bounty of the sea, but it was not to be. We had the quarry all lined up just off the port side, and in the sights of our harpoon gun. Just as the shot was to be taken, we discovered that someone had crept aboard overnight and jammed the gun. The disappointment was palpable (look it up). The coals didn't go to waste, and over a couple of hot dogs we discussed what we would have done had we tied into a several ton leviathan...

****

You're probably wondering what we're doing for Mother's Day this year. It looks like another spectacular event is being planned by some of the mothers at the club. A grand brunch will be served in the main ballroom. Following that, it is with my abstract expression of pride to announce, a gift of a large Robert Motherwell painting to be hung in the club Foyer in tribute to the many mothers in the club. This painting is a gift from the estate of our late founder, Richard Weed, who, as many of you know, died as the result of a freak jib furling accident. The ceremonies will include the ringing of the ship's bell from our beloved flag ship, the Arroyo Seco, for each mother in the club. The closing will consist of a reading of Sailing to Byzantium by yours truly, and a late showing of Ship of Fools in the club screening room.

******

Well, it is my sad duty, indeed, to report the club quarters were ransacked by vandals last night. The annual holiday display, so beloved by the membership, was befouled in the most despicable manner. As you know, we had retained the services of renowned cheese sculptor, Arthur

Chipeligo, to produce, working in veined Morbier, a nautical tableau involving reindeer and dolphins as this year's theme, to decorate the Grand Foyer of the club. Some cretinous individuals managed to break in and juxtapose these animals into the most vile postures just prior to the opening of the club's holiday bruncheon. Our apologies to the ladies auxiliary who had to discover such a scene on their arrival to arrange for this event. The incident remains under investigation....
****

The gala club Christmas party is hereby cancelled due to an unfortunate happening at an ocean park we were checking out to hold the event. Our party chairman, Rear Admiral, Stuart Gotts, was taken by a Great White while testing the waters, and the scotches. Gotts was senior partner at the Gotts, Weed law firm. His partner, Richard Weed, insisted the event go on, but a poll of the members, resulted in the cancellation.

Donations in Stu's name can be made to the club, attention: Save the Great Whites Foundation.

****

REMINISCENCES

This is a series of writings that are pretty much parts of my life that I recall thinking about in a nostalgic look-back. Recall being what it is, my recollections may be a little shaky but I believe, for the most part, they are pretty right on...

WELL, I'VE NEVER BEEN TO DENMARK, BUT I'D KINDA LIKE TO GO THERE

It was the '70s, and I was finishing up a rough divorce from my first wife. Not rough in a financial sense, but a deeply personal feeling of loss and futility sense. I was living in Pittsburgh at the time. I still remember the night I stopped on the Fort Pitt Bridge and threw my wedding band over the railing to a chorus of honking horns and revving engines behind me. Fuck 'em; they could wait a couple of minutes while I regained my freedom.

As stated, the divorce turned out to be a non-financial event. No kids and a new format of 'no-fault' divorce in a state with no alimony laws, pretty much assured me it would be just the attorney fees, etc., to get it done. However, my attorney advised me to be cautious because he had seen other divorces turn ugly at the final hearing. With that in mind, he suggested I liquidate a few assets. My biggest asset at the time, besides my cars, was a chunk of Canadian lakefront property that had been in my family for nearly fifty years. I remember hearing stories of how they had to lay down fences to drive huge touring cars over hill and dale to get there. Family legend has it that the property reminded one of my forbears of a spot in Pennsylvania from his youth. All I know is that the family gobbled up half the lakefront of a fairly large lake. After all, it was the twenties and with the oil money and stock market flying, why wouldn't you. But that's a story for another time.

So I liquidated a couple of cars and the property, which hurt me at the time, because I remembered every summer, as a kid, going 'up to the lake,' to run, swim, hike and explore. I recall thinking at the time of the divorce, what the hell, I have no kids, no wife, so why do I need a family retreat, anyway.

The divorce happens without a hitch, and so there I sit with a potful of cash. I'm getting tired of the group I'd fallen in with including the wife of a doctor, who must have defined trophy wife, at the time; anyway, she's neglected and needy. Perfect for a guy who's going through a divorce, but not so much for a guy who IS divorced, footloose, and loaded with cash. So my immediate thought turned to, of course, 'road trip.'

Not just any road trip, but something special, maybe back to Europe, yeah that's the ticket! I lived in a small German village for a year while I was in the service (Yet another story for another time) and my wife and I had been back twice since then. So Europe was my immediate thought. I needed a place to lick my wounds and think about what to do with the rest of my fucked-up life. And not just for a couple of weeks. I bagged my job and set out for a summer in Europe.

I booked on KLM to Paris with a return from Amsterdam, one of my favorite cities in the world. I bought a one-month Eurailpass, so I was all set to hit Europe and shake off a few demons. I made reservations in Paris at a fabulous place, the Hotel de L'Abbaye in the Saint Germaine Des Pres area, and I was off. What made it my ideal hotel? Perhaps it was the nostalgia of the way my wife and I found it. Oh yes, this wasn't to be a scorched earth trip, there would be a little time for reminiscence on this jaunt for sure. We were crossing into France from Germany. My wife and I, as was our practice at the time, hadn't made reservations at a hotel yet for the evening.

We came upon one of those typical 'welcome centers' shortly after crossing the frontier, and my wife went in, while I waited in the car. She came out a few minutes later with a few recommendations, but the one that really caught her eye was one offering a Grand Opening deal for this little boutique hotel in Saint Germaine Des Pres. Well, she was all for it. She had been a French major in undergrad and spoke the language fluently. Plus, at the time we were both reading a lot of Sartre, Camus, and other existentialists so it seemed like a natural. She called them and the rest, as they say, is histoire...

At any rate, I checked in, had a couple of drinks at the tiny bar, and crashed, my first night back on the continent with the whole summer in front of me.

****

We are going to do a jump-cut here to the end of that trip. I had burned through my Eurailpass, was back in Paris from a sentimental journey through Germany after a sojourn to the south of France. I decided to rent a car for the trip to Amsterdam, I always marveled at the 1st World War trenches that could be seen from the superhighway as one traveled from France into Belgium and then into The Netherlands in a matter of hours. What an existence it must have been for those men!

As is usual, the closer I got to A-dam, the lighter my mood became. There is just something about the place that makes me feel good, and I'm not talking about drugs and sex...entirely. What I love most about the city is her people. The tolerance, the love, the, I don't care what you are or what you do, as long as you are a good person attitude, is hard to define. The fact that most people, in those days, got everywhere on bikes didn't hurt either. Gone were the crazy people of the Vietnam Underground from my first couple of trips there when for a couple hundred bucks you could desert and be whisked across the border to Copenhagen, Denmark by the Provos. A time when every empty space was taken up with graffiti or signs saying, 'U Go Provo' aimed at the American G.I.s.

Did I mention Copenhagen? I had never been to Denmark except in my dreams. And I must admit, most of my thoughts were fueled by erotica where blondes were willing to do just about anything... So Copenhagen was a high priority of places to get to that summer. Ah. but first, Amsterdam. I was walking one day when I heard this incredible piano music coming from a bar that appeared to be closed. The music was something from Cole Porter being played with a deeply felt passion. It was 2 o'clock in the afternoon, much too early for such music, I made my way into the brightly lit bar, and it did indeed, appear to be closed. Chairs overturned on tables, no one in the joint, the house lights turned up, but I saw the object of my curiosity sitting at a large piano, pounding the keys diligently if effortlessly. He was a slightly built black man. He saw me immediately as I hoisted myself up on a barstool. He kind of acknowledged my presence and continued to play through the end of the song. After finishing his song, he told me that the bar was closed, but I was welcome to sit and listen if I wanted. Oh, I wanted. A short time later, a barmaid mysteriously appeared and asked me what I'd like to drink. I ordered a drink and one for the piano player as well.

He decided to join me at the bar, and my first question was where the hell did you learn to play like that. Like most talented folks he shrugged my question off. We introduced ourselves, and in looking more closely at the man, I could see he was a good 20 years older than me. He told me he was just practicing for his nighttime gig at a club where he played. I told him he had some spectacular chops and could be playing at the best nightspots in New York if he wanted. He just chuckled and told me his story, it was simple, really. At the end of World War ll, he was a Sergeant in the Army. He had a choice to make, go back to America and the hardscrabble racism he had endured in his youth, or remain in Europe where he was treated as just another human being. He said it was a hard choice to turn your back on your country, but one he never regretted. I told him my story and, as a veteran myself, I understood the conflict that arose in him but couldn't fault his choice.

We had a couple more drinks, and we found that we really hit it off, so when it came time to leave, he gave me a card with his name on it and the name of the club where he worked. He asked me to be sure and stop in to catch his act any night after 10 pm. I said I would. Man, I wish I had saved that card, the name that comes back to me is 'Cab' not Callaway of course, but his first name, or nickname, was Cab, I'm sure of that.

Over the next couple of days, I'm planning my trip to Copenhagen on the 'boat-train' as they were called. Trains that would take you to a railhead near a dock and then you and the train would be transported by a ferry boat across some expanse of water where you would continue by rail, once having crossed. The most famous, of course, being the boat-train from London to Amsterdam. All of this being moot today with the marvel of long tunnels (chunnels) and bridges. But believe me, it was important, as there was only one train per day that left for Copenhagen and it was in the early morning.

So I'm doing some day-drinking at my headquarters, Rembrandtbar on the square, and in passing, I ask the bartender, Papa, If he has ever heard of this piano player. He says he has not but tapping the card on the bar, says he has definitely heard of the 'club.' Turns out it is a high-end house of ill-repute. Not set in the red light district but on a leafy street in a very chi-chi residential neighborhood. Well, what do you know, says I, Cab is a piano player in a cat-house. So, when you go, asked Papa?

Well by then I had already booked my ticket on the train, first-class, to Copenhagen for tomorrow, so it would have to be tonight or when I got back if ever, visions of Scandinavian blondes still dancing in my head. So at around ten that evening, I am riding a taxi down the street where the club is located. It doesn't look anything like a neighborhood zoned for 'nightclubs' big imposing brownstone style front porches ensconced nicely into leaf laden walls of trees, all accented by street lights twinkling between the swaying branches. I walk up the steps to the address marked on the wall with a street number and can see through the massive double doors a gentleman seated on a stool in a foyer-like area. As I enter, he asks me what 'level' I am interested in. I explain that this is my first visit and could he give me in a little more detail what is available.

He tells me there are three levels, one is two drinks at the bar, the choice of a woman and a room on the second floor. The second is the same as the first, except it includes unlimited drinks at the bar. And the third provides dinner in their third-floor restaurant, before or after. Not being at all hungry, I opt for the first package, assuming two drinks should be plenty of time to pick a partner.

This had to be the most sound-insulated building I had ever been in including some of the world's best recording studios. The gentleman affixed a colored wristband to my arm after I paid him, and handed me off to another gentleman who took me to the parlor where he opened two sliding wooden doors, and I was immediately transported into the midst of a glossy, glitzy cocktail party lounge populated by well-dressed folks, jackets and cocktail dresses for all, and where the female to male ratio was somewhere near the 6 to 1 mark. Over in the corner, providing the soundtrack for all the partygoers, was none other than my old buddy Cab, dressed in white tie and tails, and backed by a bass player and a drummer.

He gave me a little nod of the head and a big smile, as he acknowledged my addition to the scene. I was at the bar about halfway through my drink when a cute blonde sidled up and engaged me in conversation. She had a pronounced middle-European accent. We talked for a bit. She never tried to hustle me for a drink (high-end, indeed) we might have been at a club anywhere. I asked about another girl I saw seated at the bar and without missing a beat or any show of rancor she went to the girl and, voila, the girl was standing in the place of the blonde. This girl was more to my liking, and she was a local girl from A-dam. I should have known.

Anyhow, we eventually ended up on the second floor in what can only be described as a bizarre room with a sunken whirlpool bath, a bar, and multiple screens of porno running just about anywhere you looked. I guess, just like an excellent restaurant, the

management was concerned about turnover. Later she told me she wanted to go home with me to my hotel. I'm thinking 'here we go,'
but she seemed genuine, or there was too much day-drinking that had proceeded the night's events.

The capper, once I agreed, was her telling me she couldn't just walk out with me, she might be killed. Wait, what? Therefore we had to go through this elaborate taxi deal where I go out, get a cab and wait down the street till she comes out from a side door and joins me, she has a bottle of cognac which we share on the way. We make it to my hotel, it is the wee hours, and I'm thinking, where are the damned porno clips now, when I need them.

I wake up at around 10 am, the train left two hours ago, and this girl is telling me how she has a young child and how she is just doing 'this' until..., and my head is pounding, and all I'm thinking about is how I get my money back for the train ticket. Ahhh, A-dam never change you beautiful, treacherous bitch...

****

DOWN IN WEST, BY GOD,...

This is a reminiscence. A remembrance, if you will, shrouded in the fog of a distant place, and marched to the beat of a drum that no one hears but me, anymore, I guess.

They say that humans have no memory of pain. I say that's bullshit. There is physical pain, which I believe that is somewhat true of, but what about the pain down in your soul? I think you are born with that pain because growing-up there was certainly nothing in my youth that made me melancholy or made me want to affect the 'brooding Swede' look that I did. Or, try to get just the right hunch to my back that made my popped collar look just right, and that these many years later provides me with the rounded back of an old man. You know what I'm talking about don't you, Joe Willy?

 I may not have been cool, but I was present at the birth.

Its labor pains started in the late 40's after The War. But she was ready to go by the mid-50's. And I was ready for it to be the new big brother I never had. I still remember vividly, trips down to 'Shank's Place' in West Virginia, where my forebears, ridge runners, Indian fighters, and moonshiners, for the most part, ran back and forth over the PA line like it didn't exist, which it didn't, officially, until Mason and Dixon in 1767 or so. Neither did West (by God) Virginia exist until 1863, when a dust-up over the civil war carved it out of what was then Virginia, (so there is precedence, California).

Anyway, Shank's Place was a kid's dream come true, it was as redneck-riviera as it could possibly be. It was on the curve of a dirty little creek and accessible only by a dirt road with cars that had plenty of clearance underneath. in fact, in the spring the road was hard to find, it was all growed-over as they used to say. And the nasty switchback and drop in elevation at the beginning made it virtually invisible to see coming off the two-lane blacktop feeder road. Anyway, littered along this bumpy entrance road of roughly a quarter mile, which paralleled the creek, were any number of 'cabins', vans, buses-up-on-blocks' and what have you, used as 'summer cottages' by my, unbeknownst to me, mostly ne'er-do-well extended family. Mostly extended through the Montgomery clan, descendants of the great and legendary J.L. Montgomery, oil man, par excellence... Right up until he went bust, somewhere in the 20's, I'm guessing, along with the rest of America. Took everyone with him too. Not the least of whom was Noah Moore, married to J.L.'s daughter, Nettie. Now, 'Uncle' Noah could stand on the front porch of his tar paper covered cabin which was in the far (power) corner of the property and contemplate a rock held in his hand for hours and tinker it with a small hammer, ending up telling you all about it. You see self-taught, or not, Noah was the geologist of the wildcatters that headed to Texas during the boom. God, it must have been heady times, heading on down to Alice Texas, in Jim Wells County, in search of your fortune. And rumor has it they found it too, at least a lot of mineral rights they bought up and sold before they were done.

Now Noah was the definition of cool to me, cue-ball bald, everyone else thought he was odd, but it wasn't unusual to see him standing on the little, covered porch of the 'big house' in a real Panama hat, suit pants and a vest with his white starched shirt, and old-timey, high top shoes during a thunderstorm contemplating the lightning and thunder around him. I didn't, and don't, know what he was thinking but by God, he had a Tecumseh stare that you could not, and best not try to interrupt. Maybe he was thinking how J.L. always got every check, treated his family like royalty, and squirreled money away in every bank between South Texas and NYC, along with some prime NYC real estate. According to family, he did it all with handshakes, and when the big bust came in the late 20's he was done.

Yessir, old J. L. got fucked over pretty good in the ensuing years. I think Noah made one more run at straightening everything out in the late 50's, but by then the tax people had eaten up everything. Don't get me started on Taxes. Hell, when

J.L. was in his heyday there were no taxes. Imagine that, America.

But, let's talk cool. Now Elvis wasn't shit. Back in my day, who was cool, was James Dean. One role catapulted him to the front of the line. And I'll tell you who else was cool, my cousin Wesley Mallot. Wesley, now there's a name you don't hear every day anymore. You don't hear Eugene anymore either, which was Wesley's middle name and how he was referred to - Gene, like another cool dude, Gene Vincent of Be-Bop-A-Lula fame. Gene grew up in a house with his mom, Mary Louise, an older brother, Ronnie and with his grandparents, living in the basement. Those would be Noah and Nettie. This was at their in-town address in Morgantown, just a few miles from Shank's Place.

Gene had a set of those double military brushes that pulled apart so you could brush back both sides of your hair with each hand and groom your 'duck's ass' haircut, just so. And Gene had a great DA, he had a red nylon jacket before James Dean even thought about it. A white T-shirt and jeans, set off with a pair of lived-in penny loafers, was the uniform-of-the-day. And Gene could play any instrument, and play it 'by ear', too. We used to beg him to play 'My Blue Heaven' in boogie-woogie style on an old upright piano they had. Gene was planning to follow his brother to WVU in the fall which made him even cooler to a 13-year-old idol worshiper. Mary Louise used to keep a close eye on her boys because their father was in a home (another term you don't hear much anymore) and the reason she was raising them on her own. One was never certain what she was looking for to manifest itself but whatever it was, wasn't evident, early on. She also had a couple of girls, by a second marriage, Be Be and Pee Wee by name, who were about the same age as me, give or take. They weren't kissin' cousins but I remember playin' 'Doctor' with them down by the creek at Shank's Place, maybe more than once. Good kid's, both. Mary Louise was the sensible one while her sister, 'Sis' Moore was the 'pretty' one chased after by one and all, and finally caught by Johnny Huggins, as hard drinking, and slicked up red neck as ever wore a pair of double pleated pants, with a tucked in 'Florida' shirt as there ever was. He was red-faced, good-looking, and jealous as hell. He was quite a raconteur and ladies man too. His nickname was 'Bus', short for Buster, I guess, tells you all you need to know. Anyway, they had a son, Willy, Who was a couple of years older than me, before they divorced.

So, me, Willy, Be Be and Pee Wee and a couple of other snot noses formed the ragtag cadre of pilot fish that happened to hang on Ronnie, Gene, and their pals, every nuance, and word. Out at Shank's Place. In the summertime.

It wasn't like I spent the whole summer there either it was mostly weekends when of a Friday afternoon up in PA my old man would say, damn it seems like a good weekend for Shank's Place, and off we'd go. Me and my sister, my mother and my father. Down the rabbit hole for 3 and a half hours, passing through such stellar communities as Rochester, Monaca (No, not Monaco), Burgettstown, Slovan, 'Little' Washington (The 'little' prefix just in case you might confuse that shithole with the nation's capital) and many others too numerous or humorous to mention. The family tie-in? Well, it gets a little complicated but my grandfather married Florence Montgomery, who happened to be Nettie's sister, and then Jack Montgomery, my grandmother's (Florence) kid brother up and married my mom's best friend, Ione, (another name) who lived in Pentress, WV just down the road from Shank's Place. Not to mention my grandfather was born right down another road from Shank's Place. You see where I'm headed here, right? Rednecks are thicker than thieves. 'Specially the Scots-Irish.

So, pick a summer weekend, any weekend, the kids are already dressed in our swimming togs, and we're out the door of that car and down to the creek faster than my old man can guzzle a shot with an ice cold beer chaser. Everyone is welcome and the beer and booze are plentiful. The kids are down at the creek and, what's this? Something new has been added, a serious zip line out over the creek. This was before they were called zip lines, I'm talking late fifties here. But what used to be a raggedy-ass tire swing out over the creek had been replaced with this, this engineering colossus tied high up in the trees on the one bank. And low down on the other. With a trapeze to hang onto and a pully with a rope to retrieve it and everything! This could only have been the work of Bobby Moore, Noah's son who was the smartest dude, without a college degree, in the world. Bobby stood fawning over his baby and watching as each kid took a turn sliding down to an inevitable splash down on the far side of the creek. Screaming like mad as Bobby, a pipe smoker demurely sucked on his pipe while checking the cables and huge bolts he had placed into the trees. I saw him once working on an electrical project standing on two blocks of wood because he liked to work 'hot' and he would ask me to hand him a screwdriver and laugh. I was a dumb little fucker but not that dumb.

Everything at Shank's was communal, dining and sleeping, in particular. Nettie was in charge of the kitchen in the 'big house'. and it was really a well-built house, solid as hell. but just covered in some green gritted tar paper that made it look, well, rundown. In later years I figured it was some kind of a hillbilly dodge. If you think we're stupid, why we'll just show you how stupid we can be, kinda thing. Nettie's kitchen was spectacular, the centerpiece was an old wood burning iron stove with compartments all over it, for this, that and the other. Big tables with happy faces all around. The sleeping arrangements, kids wise, was dormitory style upstairs with girls and boys separated by sheets thrown over a clothesline, and beds right up next to each other so you could crawl across the room on them if you wanted to. Everyone brought their own blankets, etc. The adult guests slept downstairs, or in their respective, ahem, 'out cabins'.

 I remember one night, in particular, after all the farting, phony cricket noises and spider scares had died down for the evening and everyone was in a deep sleep. There was a horrific crashing sound. Not like someone falling down the steps and knocking over a lamp crash, but like a fucking plane crash taking out trees in its path with a thud at the end, right outside our cabin! I swear the place jumped on its foundation. God, the initial panic was enormous, every kid expressing their own hyped up version of an alien-related idea from 'Them', the just-released alien crash-to- earth flick, to invoking the 'Flatwoods Monster' (look it up), After everyone collected their thoughts, the intrepid Mallot boys along with their pal (a neighbor from down the street in Morgantown) Bruce Lipscomb, were on the case. Ronnie and

Gene were leading the charge down the steps. The booze-addled adults were still all wha?, whoa. Except for his coolness in charge, Noah, who I never saw take a drink, and who you knew wanted to be on the front lines of this exploratory expedition, but who, for the moment, was wrapped in his bedclothes, looking a lot like Nehru, saying calmly to Ronnie and Gene, our captains of this evening, it sounded like it came from across the creek. After rounding up flashlights from the assemblage, a small group of fearless young folks set out to find out just what the hell was going on. I'm not going to kid you, as the youngest member of this expeditionary force, I was pissing my pants.

Who knew where the hell the sound came from, in the hollows (hollers), of a late night summer West Virginia it could have come from anywhere and the speculation was running wild as we jumped into Ronnie's old Nash sedan, Ronnie, and Gene, in the front, and me Willy and Bruce in the back with me as, the youngest, riding in the middle, or riding the hump. For once I didn't bitch, I was hoping they'd eat the outliers first. Armed to the tits with flashlights, and Ronnie's 1940's Nash outfitted with dual built-in spotlights, (a configuration Nash sold the shit out of in WV) we had the lumens our backbones lacked. Ronnie and Gene were of the boisterous persuasion that the crash was created by Johnny Huggins with his belly full of beer and on the prowl for 'Sis', making an imprecise turn onto the entrance road and planting his late model Studebaker into the creek. My money was still riding on some sort of extraterrestrial alien landing, but hoping like hell it wasn't. Who knew what the fuck Willy was thinking and Bruce was, apparently, just along for the ride. Boy, will they be shocked when they are the first to be eaten alive?!

I'm looking back as the lights of the house diminish, and wondering what the hell I'm doing with these dauntless explorers of the 2 am night. I'm just a kid! with Gene working one of the spots, and Ronnie the other, plus the two big flashlights out the side from our two wingmen, there was no shortage of light to mark our path through this dark night. As we approached the two-lane blacktop it became apparent that Johnny Huggins had not 'rolled' his Studebaker into the creek or over a missed turn embankment. I was happy to be on a paved highway, for now. Gene was already tinkering with the radio, trying to pick up WLS out of Chicago or, at least, CKLW out of Windsor, Ontario, when Ronnie came up with the idea of going down to the bridge across the creek and cutting back, taking Buckeye Road to the first left that would put us on the other side. then we could explore Noah's theory that the sound came from 'across the creek' Who better to read the sound waves than the sage old Noah. I didn't think it was a good idea, at all and of course, EVERYONE else in our group did. Damn, it wasn't easy being the youngest. And, of course, we had to stop in the middle of the bridge to shine our spotlights up and down the creek to discover......nothing. Double damn, we were just going to have to take the old road up the other side of the creek to find... what?

The road on the other side of the creek wasn't much better than our entrance road, but at least it was passable, And Ronnie wasn't sparing the horses as we bounced our way along it, for nearly a mile until it...disappeared! Ronnie slammed on the brakes and skidded to a halt just before crashing into what appeared to be green bushes going straight across the road. Upon a second look, it turned out to be a huge tree which had fallen and blocked the road almost directly across the creek from Shank's Place. I must admit we were all a little crestfallen as we drove back, but at least we found the source of the great crash in the night.

A few hours later the morning dawned clear and there was a heavy dew, and ground fog covering everything, not unusual at all in the hollers of West, by God, It was easy to look up and see crystal blue sky and not be able to see ten feet in front of you. The 'kids' were all up and I was regaling Be Be and Pee Wee with my derring-do from the previous evening. Just then we heard a hell of a commotion from behind the house. Very unexpected because directly behind the house there was nothing but a huge sheep pasture. Upon running out we found Lonnie

Lipscomb, Bruce's older brother, and a true bad-ass, cutting donuts in the dew covered pasture with his hot rod '32 Ford pickup truck. He had evidently come out to take Bruce home and decided to do few di-do's in the pasture first. To add to the mayhem there was Ronnie and Gene, in the back of the truck bed hangin' on for dear life as though riding a bucking bull. And loving it!

Like I said, in those days, Shank's Place was Paradise for kids. Today it would be easy pickin's for a sharp litigation attorney.

Anyhow, most of the players are dead now, but a few hang on up in them hills, except for the ones that studied the three R's: Readin', Ritin', and Route 19 the fuck outa that place!

And I'm cool with that, all of that.

****

ADVENTURES ON CATALINA

As is usual for the beginning of one of my adventures, your old Commodore, pro tem, was sitting in a bar. Le Petit Chateau in Toluca Lake, to be exact. This was a few months ago and I was with David Rogers and a group of friends, including David's daughter Nicole who was visiting from Tampa. And, again, as many of my adventures begin, the conversation turned to, "Wouldn't it be fun to...". And thus began an adventure of perilous and exhilarating highs and lows on a sail to Catalina Island.

We enlisted a couple of folks to join the three of us on our journey-
Nicole's husband, Doug Longo, a tournament fisherman, and world sailor, along with my son Grant, who lives in Philly and is an athlete and fitness freak

(and CTO of pipelinedeals.com). Thus crewed we had a total of 5 folks who could deal with anything. Despite the possibility of bad weather, we shoved off aboard the 45' Hunter, "Pied A Terre" out of Long Beach at 10:30 am and headed due south toward Avalon on Santa Catalina an estimate 4-5 hour motor/sail. Our plan was to spend one night at Avalon, more touristy, and one at Two Harbors, more rustic, about a two-hour sail up the coast of the island.

About halfway over, we called Avalon Harbor Master on VHF to seek a mooring for the night. They don't reserve in advance (as they do at Isthmus Cove) and told us the harbor was full but we could moor "out" at Descanso Beach or Hamilton. Given the weather forecast, which was worsening by the moment, we decided to divert to Isthmus Cove, at Two Harbors, rather than bounce around on an outside mooring all night. I had taken the initiative and reserved a mooring online the night before, at the isthmus, for just such a contingency.

Upon our arrival at mooring O8, Oscar 8, we found the sand line, leading to the stern hook, had been captured by a Jurassic piece of kelp which defied our ability to pull it up. We hailed the Harbor Patrol Boat and he cut away the kelp. This is when we learned these guys can be your best friend. Can't say enough about how helpful they were during our stay (more later). It was then we realized that the sand line had wrapped around the rudder. Thank, God, Grant is a big time swimmer! He jumped in with a snorkel mask and swam under the boat to untangle us. Finally, we relaxed over a few cocktails and made reservations for dinner at the Harbor Reef Club. We called the shore boat, they picked us up, and it was off to a great dinner. Which is good since the Harbor Reef is the only joint at two Harbors!

During the evening a large power boat took the mooring next to us and had tied their mooring to the starboard side of the boat. Since the weather was cool and a nice breeze was blowing, I decide to sleep on deck rather than in the cabin. Good thing I did. About 4 am something woke me up and as I opened my eyes, I was looking directly into the cabin of the large power boat, not 10 feet away. I immediately ran to the bow and stern lines, only to see that they were firm and secure. Next stop, radio to call the HP. He was out in a flash and suggested we move our mooring lines to starboard as well. He hooked a tow line amidships to hold us off the power boat while we accomplished this. Before departing he suggested, nicely, that in the future we should note how the other boats are hooked up and try to do the same.

That's when I dropped the F Bomb (to myself) and stated we were there FIRST. It was the power boat guy who made the rookie mistake, not us. HP: "Oh, then he didn't do you any favors....." Really?

The next morning, even with Hurricane Delores coming up from Mexico, it dawned clear. Not to be cheated out of a look at Avalon, we decided to proceed with our Safari Tour down the 1,600 foot spine of the mountains from Two Harbors to Avalon. We couldn't figure out why it would take two hours to go the 12 miles, as the crow flies until we were aboard the nine-person van negotiating the switchbacks on the washboard rutted dirt roads. The van had a bad front end (I kept waiting for a tie-rod to snap) and there were no guard rails and, apparently, no speed limit - yikes!

We arrived at Avalon and had a great lunch at the Galleon and as we ate we heard the booming of the thunder and the torrential downpour. We wondered if there was an earlier Safari van back to the isthmus than our 4 pm scheduled return. We checked and....not only was there not an earlier van, there was NO van! The road had washed out and couldn't be repaired until tomorrow, earliest. Uh, this being the only road from Avalon to Two Harbors, what now? The Safari company offered to put us up in a tent campsite outside of town (all the hotels were booked). We decided to explore other, and all, options. First thought, take the high-speed ferry back to Long Beach, from Avalon and then from LB to Two Harbors (about 3 hours). Too late! Next thought, since there is no ferry service from Avalon to TH (why?), Doug and I started checking out charter boat companies on the dock while Nicole, not being a big tent lady, was calling helicopter services.

When we got back from the docks to say we might have a 36' Sportfisher willing to take us to Two Harbors, Nicole was very excited to tell us that the helicopter company was willing to take us for less than the charter boat. I was calling the helicopter company to confirm when the lightning started to crackle all over the island - end of helicopter. We jumped aboard the charter fishing boat and made our escape from Avalon!

Later that same evening, we were having cocktails in the Harbor Reef and Doug was regaling us with stories of the time he was boarded by pirates off Madagascar.... Until next time kiddies...

****

WHO LOVES YOU...

This started out as a media critique blog, and while it has meandered here and there, I've tried to pull it back in from time-to-time, with at least a tie into media. In the early 70's I was the Media Director of one of the largest ad agencies in Pittsburgh, I was going through a rough divorce, knocking down chubby bucks and drinks with the stars. My office was on the thirty-somethingth floor of the US steel building in the heart of downtown. When you controlled that much money people beat a path to your door like those people in "Casablanca", desperately seeking the 'letters of transit.' Hell I even made Rush Limbaugh (Jeff Christy) cool his heels when the management of KQV (one of the few stations east of the

Mississippi grandfathered to use the K rather than the W, as the beginning of their call letters, as was KDKA) brought him in to introduce him to me as the new savior of rock and roll, in a rapidly changing music scene (see advent of Disco). Anyway, you get the picture and those of you who know me, know there couldn't have possibly been a bigger or hotter shit than me.

With apologies to the old-timey radio announcers, and to paraphrase a quote a few of you may recall, "Return with us now to those golden days of yesteryear..." Because they do seem golden. When viewed over the mist of time. Squint your eyes a little, and hell, they come back to life without the jagged edges, bumps, and bruises, just the sweet storyline. This is one of those:

I've changed his name, since he still has living family who I assume are going about their normal lives, having survived the pig-in-the-python, fame blip on their family tree. Let's just say he was a big-time media star in Pittsburgh, bordering on a national break-through. Anyway, Eddie Lamont, was Pittsburgh's answer to, who is the most eligible bachelor in town, whom I would NEVER marry, but for one night? I'm all in. Which made sweet Eddie the perfect wingman for me, I was the 'silent killer' type, while Eddie was out there. First of all, he was gorgeous in a young Tom Selleck kind of way, only better looking, (this is true) well dressed in only the best Brooks Brothers had to offer. Big mustache, tall, charming, I mean chicks fell over like a house of cards for him... Right up to the point where, later at their place, they'd catch him drunkenly pissing in a laundry basket, and cackling like a hen. You see Eddie was a drunk, a big drunk, not a bad drunk. I guess you could say we were all drunks in those days but Eddie just couldn't 'hold his liquor', which made him the perfect wingman for me.

I was living in Shadyside, a swank niche-y, little neighborhood back then and on this particular, perfect summer night I'm driving down one of those tiny side streets that give the impression you are driving through a cave of leaves, as your headlights make a perfect semi-circle through it, greenery all around. I'm on my way to pick up Eddie. Since we'd be drinking, Eddie should not be anywhere near a steering wheel! As I recall, Eddie lived in Swissvale, another tone-y (at the time) little area for the up and coming.

Now in those days, Shadyside had a small downtown section which gave a home to a number of very classy clubs. Many of them private, like the Gaslight Club. And a very hot public club called the Encore, which was owned by the (then) famous jazz trombonist (don't laugh, it was a thing) Harold Betters. And at least one 'after-hours club', the most famous of which was called the Hollywood Social Club or, the 'Soshe', to those of us in the cognoscenti, or was it the glitterati, anyway, one of those ti's. The Soshe had a Walnut Street (main st. of Shadyside) address. But good luck in finding it, if you didn't know where it was. One of the original no-sign joints, back a small alley and up a flight of outside steps with one spindly lightbulb, as I recall. But once you opened the door, oh baby, it was all happening, first class, all the way. Dining, dancing entertainment, you name it, they had it. Many times, Harold Betters, after closing his club at two, would show up to play a jam until 3 am or later. Man, life was good, baby.

But I digress, as I am wont to do.

So, we're making the rounds of the bars, we had hit the Gaslight earlier and told a couple of chicks we were headed to the Encore. While waiting for them to show, which they never did, I saw one of the classiest takedowns ever performed by a bouncer. Harold was on the bandstand with a small group playing his usual good set, when in the middle of a very crowded dance floor stood a solitary young man who seemed to have a problem with everyone and everything. He was starting to get loud and a small space was allowed around him when a nattily dressed gentlemen in full suit attire stepped up and nicely asked for him to take his problem outside, or at least lower his voice. He got louder. Big mistake. Something happened, I still don't know what, but the kid was out on his feet and stiff as a board. The bouncer moved him out as though backing out a piece of furniture on a hand-truck. Just like that. No muss, no fuss, as we used to say.

On most drinking nights, we'd be, let's say, four drinks in, and Eddie would already have attracted 2-4 of the most attractive women in the place. But by drink number five he was giving up the tell-tale signs: Staring listlessly across the room, having to be re-engaged on every new subject, etc. I tried to use the bouncer episode as a teachable moment, but Eddie was already starting to stare. We had attracted a new bevy of young ladies as the Encore was closing. We asked a couple of the more promising ones to join us at the Soshe. Apparently missing the cues, they happily agreed.

By the time we got there Eddie was already talking out of the back of his mouth, as though he were gargling his tongue. I ordered the ladies a drink and two coffees for the guys. But, Eddie insisted he 'wash'n drun' punctuated with a comically theatric hiccup and continued to drink. I think that was enough for our guests who finally high tailed it out of there. I was begging Eddie now to leave since I was his ride and his, 'Last Train to Clarksville'. "No man, serissley, that blonn chic luffs me, dude".

I didn't have the heart to tell him the blonde left 20 minutes earlier. Finally, I laid it on him, "I'm leaving you're on your own."

To which he replied, "I'm goo, man". To which I remember thinking, you certainly are…

I'm sobering up as the crisp morning mist hits me in the face as I search for my car. But, no one said being a drinking man was going to be easy. Home for a couple of hours of shut-eye, cold shower, off to work. Oh yes, kiddies work above all else. Anyhow, about 10:30 that same morning I get a phone call put through on an 'urgent' line. It's Eddie, "Dave? S'eddie, here."

"Hey, Champ didn't expect to hear from you till late afternoon, after what you put me through at the Soshe"
Yeah, well speaking of which", voice very shaky now, "I'm still here, Dave."

"No way, man the place has to be closed, I'm sure they threw your ass out hours ago. Come on, I've heard of drunken flashbacks, but......!"

"I'm telling you, I'm still here and the fucking place is empty, and all locked up. I can't get out! You gotta come and get me, man."

"Sure, sure, Eddie," playing for time, mind racing. "I can't 'break in' but you can 'break out' see what I mean."

"No, I don't 'see what you mean', this place is wired like Fort fuckin' Knox."

"Hey, who loves you, man, see you Friday night?

"Yeah, well... Maybe..."

****

OF TIARAS AND TABLETS

I was visiting my local Starbucks this past weekend, having a treat, a Flat White. It's a treat because it never fails to harken me back to the days in Europe when a Cafe Au Lait, was served from two hot silver servers, one filled with espresso, one with cream, poured simultaneously and returned to their nests of crisp linens. But, before I get too nostalgic, I must tell you of my glimpse into the future.

Now, this particular Starbucks, among the thousand or so in my immediate neighborhood, is known for hosting its share of actresses, models and other assorted courtesans (what are the odds). But this entire caffeine-acid trip started with a freeze frame of a look from one of the princesses who (used to) populate this shop. As I sat sipping my

FW, seeing and being seen, I noticed out of the corner of my eye, someone dart into the pickup counter from outside, hesitate for a moment, and pick out her order and without looking up, heading back to the door to exit. Clearly, this was a person who used the Starbucks App on her tablet to order and pay for her drink, all she had to do was pick it up and be on her way. But then, just at the door, she turned and looked at the assemblage of sippers, suckers, and slurpers. The very moment my photographic memory took the shot.

First, I noticed that she was the fairest of them all, beautiful in every way. Face, hair, and figure. Perfect. Her outfit composed of perfectly fitting mid-thigh navy blue sweatpants, the kind of fit no-one can ever find! Topped with the oh, SO-CAL layered look du jour, like a parfait sundae. A band of white tee shirt, overlaid with a band of grey tee shirt, topped with a

Lulu Lemony hoodie the color of coconut cream pie. Each band of color imperfectly layered, perfectly.

She wasn't a hothouse princess, it was clear by her carriage, more hottie than haughty. Just a gal caught up in her world, or should I say THE world

Now I'm a pretty good poker player and a fair judge of Tells. Maybe not whether you have a specific hand, but certainly whether or not you filled that straight, or pulled that third ace. Anyway, the look on her face haunts me because I saw a woman trapped in a time warp straddling her days at the student union cafeteria, yearning to see a familiar face, and a woman who no longer has time for such nonsense. I'm certain this was a woman who had a Smartwatch up one of her perfect sleeves and was probably a rising young executive at some hot silicon beach startup. But back to the look. It wasn't one of disdain or pity for the unwashed rabble at her feet. It was one of longing and regret. That was the killer part. She had all the latest ways of buying a coffee, she had the outfit, she HAD everything, but she was missing the experience! It was almost as though she had out-hipstered herself. Wham, bam, here's your latte Ma'am, don't let the door hit you in the ass.

It was a look that said, 'Wait, I was going to do my princess wave, or blow a kiss, or throw that kid a piece of Salt Water Toffee, but in two seconds, I was out the door...'

It's not too late to climb back up on the float kiddo, but that Smartwatch is ticking... and do you REALLY want to?

****

THE GREAT TRAIPSE

Wherein I travel to pre-pandemic Europe
for the entertainment of my readership...

OFF TO JOIN THE CIRCUS

Well, with two cars in storage along with all my meager remaining material goods (a friend tells me two moves is equivalent to a fire in terms of attrition of your shit), a last look out at the Verdugo's from my balcony, and I step into my Uber for the trip to LAX. Off to see my kids and grandkids on the east coast before embarking on a month's odyssey around Europe, beginning with flight into Paris and return flight from Amsterdam. In other words, Let the games begin. I hope you will follow my journey herein and from time-to-time. I will try to keep it entertaining and informative…

Let's start with my trip to LAX. My contacts deep within the Uber organization (Eddie from Glendale) tell me that Uber is not that welcome at LAX. NO legal pickups, and they are treated like Demolition Derby entrants by everyone from real cabbies to Wally Park drivers when they drop someone off there. When they leave LAX after a drop-off it looks like outtakes from "Escape From New York" with the Uber driver playing the part of Snake Bliskin.

How do the other drivers know it is an Uber Car? It is clean inside and out, the passenger and driver are both smiling, and the driver appears to have taken a shower sometime in the current fortnight.

The secret work-around, according to Eddie, is you take the Uber to a major hotel on Century Blvd., and hop one of their shuttle busses, which run 24/7, every ten minutes. Same on your return, hop the first hotel shuttle you see, get to the hotel and call for an Uber. Much more convenient than a taxi or even a Super Shuttle, really. I mean, how many times do you have to say,   'what,' to the guy running the Super Shuttle podium before realizing Rosetta Stone doesn't even have a fucking disc to cover whatever his first language is.

Because of an early departure, I stayed at the Marriott the night before, but the shuttle bus is a contract situation, they don't know, and don't care, if you are a guest there or not.

LAX, 5:30 am: The line out the door already looks like a casting cattle-call for mid-western bumpkins about to stampede in panic before a twister hits Palookaville. Only one way to handle this.

Immediately go into the terminal take the first-class line which is always empty at the check-in counter, look at no one, march to the first open agent, put your bag on the scale and plop down your papers and ID.

The burden is now on the agent. They can either look at your pathetic 'Zone 18" boarding pass with a seat next to the lavatory door and frog march you back outside to the end of the line, or, stamp it, tag your bag and say, "next", to no one. Only a slight conspiratorial glance between the two of you and you are on your way to the gate…2 and a half hours early.

As I furtively slithered past all the folks in the long line I just bypassed, I could see that they were wondering if I was some kind of VIP, an airline official, an Air Marshal, or if they should just chase me down and kill me like the fat kid in Lord of The Flies. I take solace in the fact that they could have done the same thing.

As I approached the security line I was happy I had purchased the Preferred Access pass along with a bundle of other airline amenities, like cream for my coffee. Again I skated past the lines of the great unwashed (this time legitimately) and was third in line for a new treat the TSA has come up with - the "low risk" line. A TSA officer did everything but break into a chorus of "You Can Leave Your Hat On", explaining this new system. Shoes, belts, plate in your head, nothing need be removed in this friendlier sky's approach. Not sure how they select folks for this line. I am sure the psychotic looking gentleman behind me in line had the same question, his beady eyes peering out from a ZZ Top-looking beard. No, not exactly ZZ Top, more Prisoner of Zenda.

It is my turn to enter the security scanner when I point to my knee and indicate it is more than flesh and bone. They detour me through some sort of stand-up MRI machine. Good news, I am declared cancer free, however I have to submit (ahem) to a pat down. As I left the security area, I had to admit, If the whole trip was going to be like this, I needn't have worried about whether there were any sexual encounters in my future. Hadn't even gotten on the plane yet and I was one up. I wiped the silly grin from my face and approached the food court area.

For some reason there is an elevator to the food court, which I entered right behind a couple of cleaning personnel with a mop filled cart. And, wouldn't you know, the moment the doors closed, the elevator started this erratic hopping routine, that had the cleaning lady saying out loud, "Maybe it's going to crash," to which the male half of this team stated, "Don't be saying that, now," with a look on his face I recall from a horse I used to have that had to be blindfolded to be led into a trailer. I'm sure blindfolds will be a subject at the next Airport Cleaners Union meeting.

Anyway having finally gotten to the general area of the food court, there was a huge line snaking around a corner above which was the sign announcing, Food Court, with a right angle arrow beneath it. I thought, 'People waiting in line to go into a food court'? As is my wont, I bypassed the line and saw (Aha, just as I suspected) a Starbucks mobbed beyond any reasonable capacity, surrounded by about 6 other places, open for business, offering coffee, with no lines. God, help me understand.

****

WITH THE FAMILY OVER THE 4th

Every time I land in Philadelphia I think there must be a Vinnie Fest coming up. Then I realize they are returning natives. Although these crowds are always populated and accented by a few Main Line folks who appear to be trying out for a Monty Python sketch, such as the Twit Olympics. Talk about a lock-jawed-talking group of occidental Shinto worshippers...

Two things remind me immediately that I am on the East coast. One being the humidity that comes with the summer heat. Not since stepping off the plane at Tan Sun Nhut Airport in Saigon did my clothes look so shot full of soggy wrinkles...immediately. Secondly is the traffic situation on the east vs. the west coast. Understand, that if you step off a curb on the east coast you are considered "in play". I was quickly reminded of this at the airport as I tried to cross a terminal road, at a crosswalk, only to be severely scolded by the horn of a huge Ford Explunk-a-junk bearing down on me at ramming speed. I was, truly, a deer caught in the headlights (with three pieces of matching luggage). On the west coast, Burbank at least, this guy would have been spike stripped, PIT maneuvered, dragged from his car and beaten with rubber (if he was lucky) truncheons, and taken back to HQ, chained to the wall for a couple of weeks to "think about" his community transgressions.

Or, as the chief might say, ' just who the hell do you think you are to try something as heinous as this in MY TOWN?' The cop working the airport simply said to me, "Yo, watch yourself, Bub", and looking at me as though contemplating writing ME up for jaywalking.

Once I got to my son Grant's place in the western suburbs, I immediately relaxed. He and his wife, Hally, and my 10 month old grandson Alex, are such great hosts. And to top it off, My daughter, Lindsay, and Son-in-Law Chad were in attendance, from the West Loop in Chicago, with 4 month old granddaughter, Ellie. And almost before you knew it, I was on an east coast golf course, dripping in lush summer greenery, with Chad and my other son Blake. Doesn't get too much better. The next morning, I was up early. I shagged a bagel from the bread box and opened the fridge to find we were low on cream cheese. Quandary time: do I take the last of it and say we are out? Do I take a few little dabs and leave a few little dabs? Or, do I take none, and leave it all for my loving family? Well, mystery fans?

After the 4th fireworks, and a huge cook out, it was just family again. Alex and Ellie in bed, the brace (rasher?) of Puggles (Ollie and Zoe) snuggled on the cushionback tops of the sofas, we break out the guitars.

Grant, who is the real talent (not bad for the CTO of a major CRM site) serenaded us with a few of his own compositions, some early Modest Mouse, and some Ween (his childhood musical influences). Daughter Lindsay provided some vocals I recalled from early days.

Grant lovingly handed his guitar to me and said, Pops? I did my rendition of an old CCR tune- Lookin' Out My Back Door, at which point, and at the popular request of many in the family, Grant snatched the guitar out of my hands and beat it and smashed it against the wall, a la Bluto in Animal House.

My guilt over having eaten all the remaining cream cheese, was immediately eased.

Next up: My escape into the arms of Mother Europa.

****

THE FRENCH HAVE A WORD FOR IT...

Well, kiddies, when last we spoke, I was about to escape the bounds of the fatherland and head for Europe. I am here, as you may have noticed from my FB posts. However, my blog tends to lag a few days in order for me to collect my thoughts, and my luggage. While the term Boulevardier sounds grand and fun, It has a different connotation here in France. And, I'm afraid I have turned into one. I mean, I have only been here a couple of days and already I want to strike for a shorter sightseeing week.

Anyway, the flight over was uneventful and, in many ways, less of a hassle than domestic flying. I was expecting a scene out of "Casablanca", fraught with concern over "transit papers" etc. Couldn't have been easier. Except for the hornrimmed case of B.O. who turned out to be my seat mate. Friendly little cuss he was, too, all excited, asking all kinds of questions and so on. I tried to get a look at his back to see if there was a Chatty Cathy string hanging out in order to gauge how long this might go on. Even my Easter Island Moai-head stare didn't convince him not to be a jovial chatterbox. I thought he was going to hump my leg there for minute. Needless to say, this wasn't going to work, and once the craft was buttoned up I absquatulated to an empty row of middle seats and promptly feigned sleep.

We landed at CDG, breaking through the rainy mist at about 3,000 feet. A perfect European day. I always think of Europe as brooding and grey-ish (Think Jean Luc Goddard). Or, in the mood of "La Dolce

Vita", a little off, never sunny and bright, a study in black and white. And, don't I pull the perfect cabbie for my ride into Paris.

Youngish, but looking like he is on the top of the larcenous heap of his profession.

Having done a little due diligence prior to arriving I found that the average cost of cab fare was about 60 - 80 Euros from CDG to Paris center. Since my hotel was in St. Germain des Pres, on the left bank (further south, while CDG is north) I figured, maybe closer to 80 Euros. We circled each other like heavyweight wrestlers- He trying to figure out what I knew of Paris, and me trying to discern, with feints to my cell phone and Google maps, just how far off course this son-of-a-New York cabbie was going to try take me. I pegged my FU point at 100 Euros, as he darted into every traffic jam, down every one-way, one lane alley, cursing the rain, Paris drivers, and shouting "I'm sorry's" over his shoulder at each calamitous, steering wheel pounding, set back we seemed to be encountering. When we finally got to my hotel, he said "63 Euros, please" as he lovingly struggled with my overladen bags and turned them over to the door man. I swallowed the anticipatory rage that had been building within me and turned my scornful eye toward the door man.

One thing I noticed on my tour, provided by my virtuous and loving cabbie, was the architecture. From the second floor upward of nearly every building, the influence the French had on Vietnam was marked. The first half of the 20 century was certainly a French statement of colonialism which is only apparent if you visit both countries. From the ground level to the beginning of the second floor level is where the difference is. Vietnam, particularly Saigon, total squalor, marked by the smell of rancid water, rotting jungle, and diesel fuel exhaust. A smell like no other, but if you kept your gaze above the first floor, Paris.

On my first foray out of the hotel, I played a little game I like to call, spot the Americans. It's easy, really, no matter the dress or language, the women all have their purses wrapped around their bodies in full campaign belt, bandolier mode. Looking a little like crossing guards. The men all have bulges in their front pockets where their "picpocket proof" wallets are, leaving a slack-assed look to their empty, but well worn, rear pockets where it is apparent there is something missing. No wonder the French treat us so poorly. We display to them, at every turn, our expectation of having out throats cut and being robbed. As though the only safe haven is Notre Dame, and then only if we chip in a few Euros and light a candle.

Had a great dinner tonight at La Closerie Des Lilas. Coming from a country that loves even numbers in their food choices (dozen, half dozen, brace, rasher, etc.) I found it refreshing to be offered 7 Escargot in garlic and parsley sauce. That was followed by a simple green salad, and Steak Tartare, with a half baguette of bread and frites. All washed down with a beautiful Burgundy. Best part? No clucking, on the menu or from surrounding patrons, about the dangers of raw eggs, raw meat, etc. Oh, yeah, no dessert but a great cup of real caffe au lait (shot of espresso with a hot pitcher of cream served on the side). Take that Starbucks.

A couple of random photos from my dazed wanderings...

MY FRENCH ISN'T THAT GOOD BUT ACCORDING TO
THE PLINTH (ALWAYS SOUNDS TO ME LIKE SOMONE
TRYING TO GET A PIECE OF FUZZ OFF THEIR LIP)
BENEATH IT, APPARENTLY WE HAVE CHARLEMAGNE
LANCING A BOIL ON THE ASS OF SOME NORDIC,
OPERATIC TENOR. I THINK.

THIS IS THE MURAL ABOVE THE HEADBOARD IN MY
ROOM, WHICH IS EITHER AN HOMAGE TO THE
CULTURE OF DANCE AND ARCHITECTURE IN PARIS,
OR THE HOTEL DECORATOR IS AN AFICIONADO OF
UP-SKIRT SHOTS. HEY, IT'S PARIS. YOUR CALL.

ON THE COTE D'AZURE

I say goodbye to Paris to head to the Cote d'Azure. Goodbye to my dark, pouting beauties gliding past my cafe table. Goodbye to my tough, stringy blondes walking along puffing rapidly on cigarettes. Boys with boys, girls, arm-in-arm with girls, a tall model-looking black chick from Senegal with a short, skinny Vietnamese dude in a pork pie hat. Ah, Paris. It all seems so.......American. But, it is goodbye for now as I try to beat the exodus from Paris for Bon Vacanses in August.

As I take my cab from the hotel to Gare de Lyon, we roll down the beautiful Blvd. St. Germain. Tree lined, sun dappled, fresh smelling in the morning air. Sadly, St. Germain des Pres has fallen prey (see what

I did there?), to all that is unholy. The hangout of the philosophers, writers, thinkers and artists from the past has become, uh, fat: to the left a Gap, to the right a Starbucks, a Gap KIDS for Christ's sake. And as a final stake in the heart of every existentialist, a Ben and FUCKING Jerry's. Definitely a sign of the impending apocalypse. One can only hope that late at night the ghosts of Hemingway, Camus, et al, reeling home from the Cafe Deux Magots, which I'm certain they haunt, piss on the storefronts.

Took the TGV train to Nice, 5 hours and change at 180+ MPH through the bucolic countryside south of Paris (There WAS a bullet with my name on it). Taking this trip is like taking a short course in French Economic Geography. The wheat gives way to sunflowers, gives way to vineyard. Alas, all giving way to the ugly manufacturing and shipping port of

Marseilles. But, then something magical happens as the train slows and turns east to trek along the beautiful Mediterranean coastline. The towns fluidly rattle by, Cannes, Antibes, etc., until the announcement, "Nice-Ville" (didn't Superboy grow up around here?) Unfortunately, marring an otherwise beautiful arrival, the graffiti surrounding the station in Nice reminded me a little of Trenton Station, from my NYC commuting days. I even recognized a couple of the tags. Who knew the gangs of Trenton summered on the Côte d'Azur?

Ah, well, I am ensconced at the Hotel Vendome, Just off the Promenade des Anglais and very near Old Cite. The Vendome is only three stars but one doesn't need to carry on pretenses when traveling alone. And, as is my wont, I never book more than 3 nights in advance, in case it turns out to be the Hotel de Flea Bag.

Leaving me the option of looking for a new place or begging, on my knees, for an extension as the naughty mistress d'hotel flexes her......er, uh, sorry. Got to ditch the fantasy-check app.

Had dinner at La Flore, on the Cours Saleya, last night, THE night time spot to be in Nice. The people watching was spectacular. The Côte d'Azur reminds me of "Marina del Rey, meets Malibu Barbie for a drink in West Hollywood." On a seafood diet the rest of this southern swing, it is fresh and the sauces are delicious.

Well, I am now off to lunch and to see about renting a car...

****

PIECE OF CAKE, RIGHT

Okay, let's talk about car rental procedures in Europe. This is not something you want to do, spur of the moment. Like I did. I awoke to the CNN International Channel, the only English speaking channel I get, finishing up a story on how the US is to blame for, well, everything. Laid on heavily with plummy, monotone brit accents, and all. These guys make Fox News look like NPR. Anyway, I'm laying there scratching my, er, head and deciding what to do for the next few of days. How about a few trips down the coast to explore Monaco, Monte Carlo, Menton, et al? It has been a while.

I plan to take the "tram" to the rail station (the nearest car rental place). Ah, the tram. To hear the folks in Nice describe it, it is the greatest thing since Marshal Foche (understand, they have low self esteem). It begins at a destination for tourists and ends at some ghetto I just saw on CNN....in flames. The fault of some US policy, or other, run amok, according to a slick-as-butter English news chick. The tram route was apparently designed by politicians, in league with the cab companies, since it stops exactly NOWHERE anyone wants to go. There is talk of connection with some mysterious cross-town bus route that tourists have been trying to sync up with since the first Roman Legionnaire's girlfriend sunbathed topless on the plage Beau Rivage. There is even talk the busses don't really exist.

Except I almost got hit by one late last night. It came speeding and bouncing down a dark side street like some ghost ship, its interior lights showing it to be empty, save for the ferret faced driver giving me a malevolent eye as I darted back to the curb.

Where was I? Oh, yes, renting a car at the train station.

So, this marvel of a tram takes me, one would think, directly to the train station, no? No! It drops you off, on the hottest, most humid day yet (ever?) in the south of France, at the base of the hill upon which the Nice-Ville station is built. Two blocks, straight up a cobblestone street. As I made it to the top, and the station, I recall how easy those POW's seemed to have had it building the bridge over the River Kwai. Now, soaked in sweat I find myself standing in line (Yessir, spur of the moment is the only way to travel) behind what appears to be, a number of UN delegates representing 4th-world countries. Anyway, I slowly crept toward my turn at the counter, as each transaction seemed to go through the same 16 cycles - cordial hello, a slow descent through hell, building to a crescendo of heads being slapped by palms in incredulity that Avis does NOT accept the Botswana Express Card, No, not even the Platinum Plus one.

As I was creeping up the line toward my turn to get a blast of AC through the talk-hole of the bullet proof glass-enclosed rental office, I closely observed the Avis clerk at work. He was a deeply troubled little bureaucrat, clearly beaten down by the abuses heaped upon him daily. Even his meant-to-be- jaunty, bright red Avis vest with the buffoonishly large smiley face wasn't working for him. But, by God, this was HIS cubicle and none shall pass that are not fully paid, registered, time stamped and clock punched-out, through

HIS door to the cars. I should have known this would be trouble from the moment my bright, gallic-inflected "Bon Jour" was met with a look that indicated I had just said, "You appear to be a pock-marked old hag". He continued to stare like the RCA Victor dog until I went into full beta mode indicating that I wanted to rent a car (rather than order a fucking Large with Everything) by childishly steering the rancid air in front of me. Even had to throw in an air-shift from 1st to 2nd before the little bastard would let me off the hook with a glimmer of comprehension.

It would take way to long here to describe his reaction to my request for a car (SANS RESERVE!?) Suffice it to say, After a number of, apparently hilarious, phone calls and in-cubicle conferences with his fellow workers, also filled with jocularity, he indicated he MAY have a car he could let me have...

Time to get down to business, his beady eyes flicking about as he pulled paper after paper from some overstuffed folio, file, or other rathole, brimming with forms.
 Yellow ones, pink ones, blue ones, all cobbled together, stapled and time stamped (bet your ass) and presented along with a blast of AC through a briefly opened hole in the glass. Quickly slammed shut with, I believe, just a touch too much glee.   I filled them out and gave them back with my international and California drivers licenses, both of which he held at arms length, with a look as though I had just presented him with a stalk of rotten bananas. Then his look changed, as a bushy, caterpillar-looking eyebrow severely arched over one of his porcine beads, he looked at me and said, with one last look at my license, and a deeply accusatory sigh, "Am'MONS?", in a tone that indicated this was the most

preposterous fake name he had ever heard in his long, sad lifetime of renting cars. Finally, we get through the process. I am standing there with a sheaf of papers representing more pulp than the Treaty of Versailles, and THEN, he tells me the cars are not actually HERE, non, non, non (you damned fool), but two blocks over, and 6 flights up a parking garage. My mention of a Courtesy Bus set off another round of mirth within the cubicle. (Teach these Americans to burn down MY ghetto!). I slog the two blocks, 6 flights and I am off on another adventure.

Next time, the RETURN of the car....

****

FOR HE IS THE DUKE OF EARL

I know I owe you the end of the car rental story (the return) but I just have to interject here a note about the vaunted "Mediterranean Diet". I'm not sure why they vaunt it, but I can tell you it is great. Yesterday, sitting by the sea, I had a salad with copious amounts of oil and vinegar, followed by broiled sea bream with more fries and bread than you can shake a baguette at. Oh, and the waiter seemed to be appointed directly by the Obamacare Commission to see that my resveratrol limpids remained topped off. I don't know about you, but if these folks are living longer by eating like this, I'm all for it.

Ah, but back to our story. So I'm ready to bail out of the south of France and I return the rental car as they (he) asked, to the 6th floor of the parking garage at the Hotel Isis two blocks from the station. My walk back to the station to complete the paper work taking me through a gauntlet of beggars, hookers and mutual fund salesmen. And then I am back at the scene of the original crime. You would think there would be a return "express" line, but, again, non, non, non. The same little wart, sitting on his same little bullet-proofed, air conditioned tuffet was in charge, with all the same tics, gestures and mannerisms on full display. Stamping away at massive sheafs of paper, as though every rainforest was his personal enemy to be waded through, and killed, daily. If only his ink pad supplies could hold out (Sarge, we need more ammo up here, we're being overrun...!). So, I'm in the same sweltering line to return my car that I was in to rent it, but this time there is only one guy in front of me. And he seemed to be speaking some form of English.

But it is that bitchy, whiney, arrogant English that only they can pull off (See: Michael Caine in "Alfie"). Apparently he wants a car (with no Reserve!?). He is sent to the "bad chair" by Mr. Avis to await the return of a car by someone (Hello. Me, here). When I step up to the talk-hole for that refreshing blast of AC, I can see the desperation on the little guy's face. He indicates that the gentlemen sitting right over there is waiting for a return car so that he can rent it. He is perhaps some sort of royalty, my red vested host implies. I, for one, don't give a crap if he is the Duke of Ellington and indicate so by yawning and leaning on the counter, gulping free AC while fixating on a mustard stain on the clerk's red vest, for which I am certain his supervisor has already done the French equivalent of ripping him a new one. This seemed to discomfit the little guy, which is why I continued to stare at it.

Anyway, I slide my papers under the hole meant for paper sliding, again, which delivered a nice blast of AC and which was, again, slammed shut immediately, lest I get too much of a contact chill. The dude begins an immediate stamping fit during which I swear, amongst the papers, he stamped the back of his own hand and the tip of his tie, which overhung the counter. Ah, but now the coup de grace. With his little bunny nose quivering, his beady eyes focused on me, his final stamp hovering, the 4th Duke of Earl breaking his imaginary bonds and rushing over to take posession of the coveted Toyota Yaris, mister red (and yellow) vest asks, "Auto is bon"?

I parked the car two blocks and six flights away and he's asking ME, if the car is okay. I saw a power opening and I took it. My drawn out, "Well, come to think of it...", saw the collapse of the Duke and a look of incomprehension (by now I know it is his default look) spread over the face of mustard vest. Afterall, in a speed read of French when I picked the car up, I was asked to sign off on the car. He could have been telling me there was a dead man in the back seat and he had to remain there over the course of my rental period. I signed. So, now with the tables turned, his stamp at mid hover, the Duke clasped around my ankles with a pleading look, like one of Wellington's men at Waterloo, I gave my rapid fire run-through in English.

"Well, you see, you know the Moyenne Corniche and that hairpin turn at Cap Ferrat, the blind one? Yes, well you see, there was a lorry coming the other way and he forced me off the road. I didn't realize there was no shoulder and I shot off a cliff. Thank God for all the pine trees that broke my fall."

The Duke was listening now and the clerk had lowered his stamp, slightly.

"Anyway, the pine trees broke my fall causing me not to hit the water as hard as I might have otherwise. Surely the orphans having a picnic on their pontoon boat would have suffered much more severely had I struck them dead-on, rather than causing their craft to merely capsize. No harm though, the tykes seemed to enjoy the diversion, and the cooling dunk. I managed to flag down a fishing boat which was kind enough to drag the car up and drop it close enough to the beach where I could push it back on the road. From there it was a piece of cake. Got the car back to the hotel, grabbed some towels from my room and buffed out the pine needle scratches. Oh, and the room hair dryer worked wonders on the interior."

The Duke, who understood every word, "But, you can't expect me to take this car...."
Mustard Vest, "C'est bon, oui?"
"Oui," Clonk went the stamp. She's all yours, Duke!

****

WE'LL ALWAYS HAVE PARIS (FOR THE MOST PART)

Well, I used to always say Paris had a certain je ne sais squat. But, either I've softened or Paris has because for the first time ever in my life, leaving Paris (and I have left more than a few times, with many different motivations) I feel a little melancholy. Paris has lost its sharp elbows, or perhaps I have become less sensitive, not sure. But, they really do speak english with no resentment now. And they don't belittle my efforts of trying to speak french. In fact, they encouraged it. Every time I got a word correct, they threw me a piece of croissant.

But, seriously, it has to be generational. The younger ones breeze through english while the really old ones resent it. Maybe that is what it was always about, the older generation resenting the younger and too embarrassed to give in. Anyway, I'm glad they have, and we are meeting in the middle, particualrly in Paris. It used to be that you had to go to the Cote d'Azur to get by with english. They seemed to understand upon which side their baguette was buttered. But, not just that. I think I have mellowed. No more rage to be The American. No more kicking out taxi windows in fare disputes and having to be rescued by the concierge. Oh, yes, it happened, in a place and time far, far away. But, again, I have mellowed and this is my farewell tour, if you will. So Let's just say almost everything has been forgiven. From my perspective, for the most part.

Anyway, back in Paris from my sojourn to the South and once again ensconced at the Hotel de l'Abbaye, on Rue Cassette, my Paris home, and where I bonded with the concierge (see above) back in '73, I decided some touristy activities might be in order.

Decided to take a long stroll to the Musee d'Orsay, which has always been one of my faves. Beautiful summer morning stroll until I approached the museum. I could tell I was close because I saw their pole sign, with their three iconic mascots atop. Manet, Monet and Jacques. Under which was their slogan: "The impressed like us, the impressionists love us". I thought the line to get in seemed light so I didn't bother with the preferred entrance fee. Ha. Paris has been taking lessons from Disney: Hide the line inside the building so when the sap gets in there he is immediately sucked into a quicksand-like serpentine line from which there is no turning back. They got me good, there.

So, I get inside, and one of the first big signs inside the Musee is the NO LIST with circle slashes over cameras, cell phones, cell phone cameras, food, drink, pets, meat of any kind, real fur, fake lizard skin cowboy boots, etc. etc. So, barely inside the door, some American with a greasy sandwich in one hand (I'm certain there was meat involved there) and a high-end Nikon, with rapid fire flash attachment, is running a panorama shot around the place. People are diving for cover, not certain if we were under attack or if there was a pop-up typhoon that was striking. Needless to say, black suited security dudes materialized in a slo-mo strobe-effect caused by the guy's flash equipment, and Rodney Kinged his ass, before perp-walking him out the door. I didn't even get a chance to ask him if he was done with his sandwich, which was lying there next to a crushed paper cup and a pool of Pepsi, which I'm also pretty sure was his. Damn, I should have eaten before hand.

The joint is pretty much as I remembered, with the big time impressionists upstairs and a few at the lower level to keep you interested as you make your way upward. Some pointless Pissarro pointilism pieces, depicting, I guess, how he discovered dot matrix printing before anyone knew what it was. But, like a movie poster, you can't stand too close or the cleavage on the starring actress just looks like a bunch of dots.

The other thing they hit you with, a lot, is death. The "Death of Arthur" (Mort d'Artur). They have a whole room, which I call the Mort hall of fame, dedicated to Mort. For all the priest's, saints and religious figures depicted during that time in history, there seemed to be a lot of Morting going on.

****

.

With apologies to Geoffrey Chaucer, I offer -

A MONK'S TALE

This is a story I tell which is about a company of wartime helicopter pilots and their beloved mascot, a monkey named BJ. Bittersweet in that even though it is fiction, many of the characters existed and I can still see them, if only in my mind's eye...

I believe all the players are dead now, either through enemy action then, or through the sandstorm of time. So, I thought I should get to putting down a few of my memories before a grain of sand with my name on it catches up with me.

Now, In 1967 Republic of Vietnam, many aviation outfits had a monkey, or two, in residence. And as you might imagine, when you add a monkey to the mix it usually adds up to war story. This is one of those.

Monkeys are native to Southeast Asia along with tigers, elephants and other assorted weird-assed birds, reptiles, and mosquitos big enough to stand flat-footed and fuck a farm-raised turkey.

This particular remembrance, among many from those times, is about one of those monkeys. A very special monkey named BJ. Before you jump to any conclusions about the meaning of the initials, I will tell you it was short for LBJ, a monicker the press stuck on Linden Baines Johnson. So, in that sense, BJ was a living tribute to the esteem in which our boys held their political and military leaders of the time.

Life expectancy of a combat helicopter pilot in a war zone is relatively low. Somehow, like them, BJ knew the odds, and also like them, was determined to have an outrageously good time while it lasted.

BJ was the mascot of the 108th Assault Helicopter Company stationed at Duc Phu, AKA, Duck Fuck. More specifically, BJ was the mascot to the pilots, or 'aviators', as many in the army preferred their flyers be called.
BJ became the company mascot when he was bought during a drunken debauch in

the local village about six months previous by Chief Warrant Officer, William "Wild Man" McGinty. At the village black market a young macaque was in a mid-range of purchase-difficulty. Somewhere between pussy, and a still in the crate Jeep with a turret mounted .50 caliber machine gun (Gasoline and ammo not included).

McGinty was one crazy son-of-a-bitch. No idle tribute, given the company was loaded with crazy sons of bitches. Like the time McGinty took a Huey gunship up at night and strafed the mess hall because the Mess Sgt. wouldn't put steak and eggs on the breakfast menu. Cookie got the message, but McGinty was dead before he got to order up, or be called into account. Shortage of aviators being what it was in those days, the brass allowed McGinty to continue flying until they decided what disciplinary action should be taken against him for the incident.

McGinty died two days after embarking on the 'breakfast war' when an artillery round (one of ours) caught his gunship square in the belly, killing all on board. They patched up the mess hall and named it after McGinty in a moving memorial service, Photos to wire services, personal effects to family, McGinty Mess Hall sign over the door in perpetuity. Perpetuity not lasting as long as it used to, one of our pilots took a trip back on one of those nostalgia, deals in the '90's. Says a clapped-out old papa-san laughed insanely and pointed to a clearing in the jungle outside the village where the runway used to be. The site of the mess hall, and all else, reclaimed long ago by the relentless jungle foliage.

BJ was the Wild Man's legacy to the outfit and the young monkey had since taken up hanging out in whatever hooch had the action on any given night. Card games, dirty movies, war story sessions, whatever.

He usually returned each night, however, to sleep on a woven palm-frond-mat, lining a platform perched in the bamboo rafters above McGinty's old bunk. All the hooches had names, and McGinty's was referred to as the Lair. The perch was built for BJ by the Wild Man right before his untimely departure.

Although, come to think of it, no departure in Vietnam was ever considered untimely or surprising to any of the players. I really believe combat helicopter pilots were a modern-day cult of stoics. Absolute steel when the pressure was most intense, with an emotion pool about a quarter an inch deep, at least when the action was hottest. The army screened them that way before they could ever get into flight school, young, intelligent, athletic and aggressive. So, basically, cool nerved smart-assed, thugs with a sense of humor.

The intensity of combat flying requires complete emotional discipline. So it wasn't surprising that monkey business was the first priority when the day's missions were completed.

Anyway, BJ, was a horny little monk, with a penchant for just about any orifice, animate or otherwise, with which he could slake his desires.
He eventually had to settle for inanimate, as he began to understand that members of the outfit had a total lack of desire for intimate contact with him. This lack of desire had been clearly communicated by various means. From gentle but firm shoves, to a final "I got it" coming from a size 12 jump boot. With a toe-shot to the chest, sending BJ over a bunk and into an open wall locker. The kick left him with his wind knocked out and in a heap of combat boots, flip-flops, and back issues of Gent magazine, his ardor somewhat deflated.

That's not to say there wasn't genuine affection for BJ among the men. They loved the little bastard, as long as he was not pulling a caper related to humping one of their limbs or possessions.

Still, there were occasional flareups when newer people would enter the mix. People that had not yet been tested by BJ. And BJ was a tester. Always looking for possibilities turning his head sideways scratching his nuts, analyzing, gauging. Looking for an opening so to speak. When BJ was pursuing his libido-driven interests he was devising other attention-getting hi-jinks which he knew delighted his jaded audience of battle weary aviators. A natural born class clown, BJ was always playing to the crowd. A ploy he knew added to his longevity as outfit mascot. Why else have a monkey, he reasoned? Indeed?

Well, like I said, BJ was a tester and like any lothario worth his testosterone, BJ wasn't about to let an FNG (fucking new guy) slide by without at least an attempt at amore. Unfortunately, the newest of the FNG's was the newly appointed Executive Officer of the outfit, Major Hagan. Doubly unfortunate then was the fact that Hagan was a paper pounder.

Unrated, i.e. not an aviator, no wings on the chest. While this usually made for a good XO, it also made for no respect or compassion from the aviators he helped command.

His type was ripe for all sorts of mayhem and merriment for the general amusement of the troops. Or, as CWO Buzz Caldwell put it, Hagan was definitely, "In play".

BJ's primal instincts sensed the lack of regard with which the men held Hagan since the new XO's first visit to the Lair ended in infamy for the 108th and became the stuff of officers club legend and lore throughout the army.

But, I'm getting ahead of myself. We need to fill in a few things here about the players before we get to the "Hagan incident." The aforementioned Buzz Caldwell was a major influence in the life of BJ and the antics associated with the outfit in general. Caldwell was a world class prankster and practical joker from some dying steel town northwest of Pittsburgh, PA. He used to refer to his hometown as West Bumfucked, PA, but it might have just sounded like that.

You couldn't tell with Buzz, because if he wasn't fucking with you out-right, he was probably setting you up for something later. He could also spot a pompous asshole in desperate need of being mocked. He had the same unerring eye as a hawk locking in on a crippled field mouse. The thing that really made him a successful practitioner of the practical joke, was that he had chiseled good looks with big blue eyes and crewcut blonde hair. It gave him the pure, innocent look of a small town hick. As one of the guys put it, Caldwell could short-sheet your deathbed and get away with blaming it on your mother.

When the flying day was over and there were no night missions laid on, Buzz would usually be in the center of the evening's social activity on the improvised deck tacked onto the front of the Lair. It was understood by all that cocktail hour started at the Lair before going over to the Prop and Rotor, as the officer's club was called, for more serious drinking and a rehash of the day's missions. Dinner was optional.

The deck was strategically positioned to oversee all the activities on the company's main thoroughfare, with command post at one end, and the operation's shack at the other end of the officer's hooches. There were eight officer's hooches, each containing living arrangements for six aviators. The hooches were lined down one side of the graded dirt road that formed the company "street". On the other side of street were the showers, and a large outdoor latrine building.

The showers consisted of a square wood platform with upright two-by-fours attached to it. There was a canvas wrap extending all the way around, providing some privacy.

The wrap started 18 inches above floor level to allow for cross ventilation and to help prevent mold and mildew. This facility was considered luxury since the post at Duc Phu did not have plumbing as such. The apparatus consisted of two shower heads attached to two salvaged wing-tip fuel tanks, mounted atop the simple structure. The tanks were painted black to absorb the sun's heat during the day. The tanks were refilled nightly by the FOD squad from a water tank truck. More about the FOD squad later.

Also, on the other side of the street was a latrine, and a good old-fashioned outhouse it was. Inside was a utilitarian "six holer", six holes cut in the bench-like shelf with each hole having a traditional toilet seat affixed to it. Toilet paper was not on rollers, but more communal with a few rolls sitting between the holes.
Behind the scenes or more precisely, below the scenes, under each hole there was a 55 gallon drum, cut in half around the circumference, sitting under each hole to catch the droppings.
The lower quarter of the back outside wall was on piano hinges creating a large flap,

allowing it to be raised so the drums could be dragged out, contents doused with kerosene, and burned every couple of days when the wind was blowing out at Wrigley, as we used to say. You did not want to be downwind. This task was also accomplished by the FOD squad.

Ah yes, the FOD Squad. FOD, in aviator speak, stood for Foreign Object Damage, caused by the ingestion into a turbine engine of some small loose object, or debris. In other words, any unauthorized, undesirable object, which could fuck up the works was referred to as FOD.

Thus, the FOD squad was a group selected each week from a group of enlisted men designated as fuck-ups, or who needed to be disciplined for various minor infractions. These generally ran the gamut from screwing up their assigned duties, to getting the clap from one of the village 'mama-sans'. The length of stay on the squad depended on the severity of the infraction, anywhere from a couple of days to a week or two. Thus they were relegated the task of burning shit, filling shower tanks, and generally handling all the least popular, but necessary, daily details of living in the tropical paradise that was Duck Fuck.

Well, anyway, Buzz was in full party swing with a group of the aviators on the deck of the lair. Drinking, bullshitting and re-flying the day's missions were the main activities. The mostly good-natured ribbing of various company members heading across the street to the showers or the shitter was also on the agenda.

Buzz, and others, punctuated their cocktail conversations with shouted observations and comments directed at those headed across the street in various attire. A trip to the showers meant you were wrapped in a towel, wearing flip-flops, dog tags and a hat. The ever present Colt .45 automatic tucked in a shoulder holster dangled from one arm completing the look which seemed to be the uniform of the day for shower-bound pilots. The hat and pistol were placed on a hook outside the shower entrance.

A trip to the shitter usually called for something a little more formal. Fatigue pants, T-shirt and a copy of Stars & Stripes, or letters from home, or from "Penthouse". The protocol in these matters was fairly off-hand.

The reason for being armed with a pistol at all times was that a sudden mortar attack followed by a ground assault was always a possibility.

A breach of the airfield perimeter was not uncommon. Once through the perimeter, a "sapper" could wreak havoc with a bag of grenades and an automatic weapon. Firing on the run and spewing grenades like a homicidal Johnny Appleseed until someone cut him down with a .45 or sawed-off 12 gauge. The life of a sapper had a few drawbacks that Ho Chi Minh may have forgotten to put in the recruiting brochure. Classic jokester, that Uncle Ho.

All travelers to the other side of the packed dirt street had to pass the deck of the Lair, which not only faced the street but was next to the only bridge across the 6 foot deep runoff ditch, which paralleled the street. The bridge was made of two pieces of pierced steel planking (PSP). PSP was usually used to build makeshift runways over soft ground. In this case two scrounged pieces were laid side-by-side across the ditch providing a narrow passage to the other side.

Most of the year the ditch was dry but you still needed to use the bridge to get across since it was over 6 feet deep.
During the monsoon season, which was currently raging full-tilt-boogie, torrential afternoon showers usually flooded the ditch to overflowing for a few hours each day until the sun returned as though nothing had happened. As a result a pole affixed with a small company pennant was used to mark the location of the bridge which was under an inch or so of dark muddy water during overflow periods. There was a marker pole on each side of the bridge. The poles were anchored to old jeep wheels.

As Captain Black, attired in shower uniform, felt with his feet for the bridge while holding onto the marker pole, buzz looked up to comment on the purple towel wrapped around the captain's midsection.

"Hey Blackie, did your mother send you that towel or did you steal it from the from the Turkey Farm?"

Buzz's comment brought laughter from the assembled imbibers and a scream from BJ, who was reacting more to the response from the others than to any understanding of the comment, or what might be appropriate in a war-zone towel. I think.

The Turkey Farm was what the boys had dubbed the Ritz Steam Bath in the village. At the Ritz you could get a steam bath as well as a massage from an enterprising young mama-san. Reason for the Turkey Farm name however, was that for a few extra Piasters you could get "gobbled" as part of the massage. It was more than once intoned, I think I'll head into the Turkey Farm for a steam job and a blow bath.

Following Captain Black, was commanding officer of the 108th, Colonel James Madison Martin, affectionately known as Marty. Marty was a fellow aviator and though he had to make tough, not always popular, decisions he had the respect of the men.
The main reason for that respect being that Marty would always pencil in his own name on the tough missions, as one of the pilots. He wasn't a 'hangar commander'.

Marty stopped by the deck and leaned on the railing-top and addressed Buzz specifically, but everyone in general, "You know we are in-processing Major Hagan tomorrow and I want to have him visit the hooches tomorrow night after missions for a little informal introduction to the company. Get a feel for how we live, and to meet each of you in your habitat, so to speak. Feel free to have some snacks and drinks on hand, just a typical night after work type of thing. How does that sound?" Caldwell looked around the assembled group and said, "Sounds great, sir. Sorta like the Queen Mother trooping the home guard"?

Marty gave a short laugh and said, "Look, let's all be on good behavior tomorrow and see if we can get off on the right foot. Major Hagan comes highly recommended and is a superb administrator, just what I need to keep you yahoo's straight.
I know he isn't flight rated but that is not why he is here. As you are painfully aware, we have a shortage of rated officers at commanding rank levels. It's a reality of this war and I don't want his lack of rating to be an issue for this unit." Marty raised his eyebrows and hesitated for a moment then added the obligatory, "Am I clear?"

Buzz acted hurt, replying with, "Marty, you know us better than that."

Marty gave a looked that implied he knew them only too well. He began to reply then just nodded and continued to the showers.

Buzz surveyed the assembled and said, "Great, just what we need a fucking tea reception for the FNG." He got generally negative acknowledgment from around the deck as he poured BJ a little more of the monkey's favorite drink: Banana Rum Madness. A drink Buzz invented and which usually added to the intensity of BJ's capers.

Buzz returned to his conversation with Tony Delvecchio, who everyone referred to as Dago. It was odd how ethnic and racial issues didn't count for much in the 'Nam. An ethnic slur that would get you killed in the states was a bonding element in a war zone.

"So, Dago, you were telling us how you ended up becoming a helicopter pilot and eventually becoming involved in this left-handed, Bohemian jug-fuck called Vietnam".

Delvecchio replied,"Yeah, well, I got fascinated by helicopters when I learned that they were first conceptualized by Leonardo da Vinci in some of his early drawings. You know, da Vinci was Italian like me. That impressed me so I started studying up and one thing led to another and, as they say, here I am.

Buzz thought for a second and said, "I thought the Italian connection was because the rotor blades slapping the air went wop, wop, wop?" Bringing more howls from the evening's revelers.

"Fuck you, Caldwell," Said Delvecchio, laughing in spite of himself.

Buzz and Dago had the kind of camaraderie born of combat. In one of the earliest missions for both of them, they were flying together when a lucky shot through the engine followed by a forced landing, stranded them in a rice patty. While waiting for rescue they exhausted all the ammo on board holding off a determined squad of NVA regulars which was closing in on them. They were fighting with trench knives when the gunship answering their May Day drove off the remnants of the squad that Buzz, Dago and the door gunners had already done a fairly good job of killing or maiming. One door gunner was killed the other seriously wounded. Buzz and Dago were both wounded by flying plastic and metal shrapnel caused by rounds zipping through the aircraft. From that day forward they were like blood brothers.

While Buzz and Dago continued to talk, a couple of other Lair inhabitants, in anticipation of the return of Captain Black from the showers, were busy moving the poles marking the bridge crossing the drainage ditch, about 2 feet to the right of the original moorings. Not enough for anyone to really notice.

As was typical on a monsoon afternoon, the muddy water from the daily downpour obscured any trace of the PSP footbridge. The cocktail crowd on the deck busied themselves trying to look nonchalant as Captain Black strode purposely from the showers lighting up a post-shower cigar. BJ, jacked up on Banana Rum Madness, and seeming to understand exactly what was about to take place, gave a couple of screams and climbed a hooch support beam to get a better view of the coming event.

Captain Black approached the bridge and began a cursory feel about with his flip-flop clad right foot covered up to the ankle with swirling water while keeping a steady bead on the marker pole on the other side to ditch.

He gave a momentary expression of tactile recognition and took a big step into the water disappearing instantly as though yanked by the ankles. His hat and cigar remained afloat and were swiftly carried downstream. Captain Black was under for quite some time but came up downstream sputtering and furiously clawing at the near bank. A crowd of seemingly concerned helpers began to pour off the deck, expressing confusion as to how he could've possibly missed the bridge. They dragged him, coughing and sputtering, to his feet while Buzz and Dago, now behind a mud covered Captain Black, moved the poles back to their original positions.

Black was shouting, "I know someone moved that pole, God dammit that pole was moved!" By now Buzz and Dago had joined the crowd around Black. Buzz said, "Captain I think you're wrong there. Why, we were out on the deck the whole evening and the Colonel himself just went across a few minutes ago.

We would've seen anyone who tried to move it. I think your footing was just a little off this evening".

Captain Black, not believing it for a moment, scanned the faces around him as he turned to go back to the showers and clean himself up, "You bastards," was all he could think to say.
As he passed the colonel, who was returning to his hooch, the colonel said, "What the hell happened to you, Blackie?" The Captain continued walking to the shower mumbling to himself and shooting

a look in the general direction of the deck. Colonel Martin shook his head and gave an 'I don't want to know' look towards the men on the deck as he continued to his hooch.

The rest of the gang began packing up to head for the Prop & Rotor for a continuance of the proceedings.

Once at the club, Buzz, Dago, CWO Eddie Sizemore and Lieut. Tyrone Hoskins chose a table and actually planned to eat dinner. A move that brought more than a few stares in the direction of the normally heavy drinking quartet. A long day of flying was laid on for the next morning which made the choice easy. They were all totally irresponsible about everything except their flying duties and their total loyalty to each other. Hoskins was one of the few black pilots in 'Nam and well-liked enough to be teased unmercifully about it. In fact, Buzz was so taken with the fact that Hoskins made it through flight school, primarily populated with redneck instructors, he figured he must've been an incredibly exceptional flying talent, which he was. And which prompted Buzz to dub him, one drunken evening, 'Super Pilot.' The only part of the name that stuck was 'Supe'. Sizemore was a doer, hardly ever talked, but always in the middle of everything. It was Sizemore who initiated the move of the bridge marker pole, which the group was still chuckling over and replaying the details as they walked down the steam-table line of dinner offerings.

"That simple minded motherfucker went down like he was hit by a shark," said Buzz, as he loaded his plate. "Sizemore you are an absolute goddamned genius."

Sizemore looked embarrassed and said, "Awww, I couldn't have done it without Supe. He helped me move the wheel rim.

That damned thing was heavy, specially with the water weight, and it was stuck in the mud, too!" Buzz nodded, "Hey, buddy, that's what combat is all about. Teamwork!"

When they were seated Dago turned to Buzz and said, "Hey man, tell the truth, you were flying second-seat the night Wild Man did the mess hall, right?"

Buzz looked up and said, "I cannot tell a lie, I was working the guns. McGinty was so fucking drunk, I had to set the G lock on his shoulder harness to keep him in the seat."
"I had to go with him to keep him from killing himself, or anybody else. I knew that no one was in the mess hall at that hour. I just put one quick squeeze through the tin roof for minimal damage, but which absolutely delighted Wild Man. When we got back, I low-crawled away from the

aircraft with BJ on my back." Looking stunned, Supe said, "BJ?"

Pausing for full effect, Buzz said, "BJ. It was the night he won his wings. Little fucker's been up a few times since then too."

"I'll be damned," said Sizemore. The other two just shook their heads and rolled their eyes. But Buzz was feeling expansive and allowed the group to talk him into telling the full story of what led up to the mess hall strafing....

A few days previous to that night McGinty and his crew had been assigned a mission of helping out with the evacuation of a village near the Parrot's Beak, in the Iron Triangle region, northwest of Saigon.

The village was being evacuated because artillery was going to level it for being in the middle of the Ho Chi Minh trail into Vietnam from Cambodia. The village was sort of a rest stop at an exit ramp. It had to go. Anyway, the South Vietnamese farmers who inhabited the village were told they were being taken to a resettlement camp. They were told to pack up all belongings and be ready to be airlifted out.

'All belongings' to a South Vietnamese farmer usually included a water buffalo for plowing and heavy pulling. The crews could easily handle the chickens, pigs, cats and other assorted small animals but a water buffalo presented a formidable task, since it wouldn't fit inside any of the assembled craft. Even if it did fit, no one wanted a two ton, pea brained, pair of bellowing horns inside an aircraft.

As it turns out, McGinty and Caldwell were flying a D Model Huey that day and one of the door gunners was 'Slicky Boy' Dobbs, a Spec. 5 crew chief who had rigged sling configurations to haul everything from Nguyen Cao Ky's limo, to part of a double-wide trailer doing duty as a portable whorehouse. Hell of a rigging resume. Used to working under fire in hot LZ's, he wasn't going to be stumped by a water buffalo with an aversion to being gift wrapped and taken to 2500 feet, no siree.

Slicky Boy sat on the floor of the parked Huey watching several other chiefs try to wrap the buffalo with some sort of sling configuration so that it could be externally lifted by a chopper. Finally, he walked over to the frustrated group trying to subdue the frightened animal. The load riggers were surrounded by a gaggle of shouting papa-sans and other advisers, none seeming to have the key to packaging the load. He cut through the group and said, "Blindfold it". Everyone was so surprised by the simplicity of this obvious idea that the hubbub came to a stop as a couple crew members used shirts tied together to accomplish the task. McGinty and Caldwell had the cockpit doors of the idle aircraft open for ventilation and sat back in their seats to watch Slicky Boy ply his trade while they sucked on a couple of Marlboros. It was about as relaxed as pilots got while they were in 'Indian country'. They rarely strayed far from the cockpit in case Charlie tried to take a run at them with his mortars, snipers or even a human wave assault. They were used to Slicky Boy's magical abilities with awkward loads and got a kick out of him as he took charge of the ragtag group of wranglers.

"Okay", shouted Slicky Boy, "forget those sling wraps and lay a cargo net out flat on the ground." A couple of men laid out a net and Slicky Boy deftly took hold of the buffalo's tether and slowly, but firmly, waltzed the blindfolded animal onto the net.

"All right now, gently fit his feet through the netting and gently pull the net up his legs, gathering as you go." The subdued beast was soon wrapped in the cargo net with Slicky Boy holding the ropes attached to each of the four corners and forming them into a single loop, which could be attached to cargo hook on the bottom of the aircraft. He turned to face the Huey and raised both his arms, like an entertainer seeking applause for a just finished dance recital, heaving chest and all.

McGinty said ,"What a fucking show boat. He's slicker than a fucking towel boy in a Tu Do street whorehouse." Caldwell waved his arm at Slicky Boy as though to say, 'get the fuck out of here,' which is what he said. Slicky Boy had another of the wranglers hold the ropes together and raced over the parked Huey. "Come on sir, fire this puppy up we'll have that yak, or whatever the fuck it is, outta here and be at the camp before dark!"

Caldwell yelled,"Clear!", and McGinty began to crank the turbine as Slicky Boy ran back to take control oh the reins of his load. The Huey came to high hover and began to position itself over the load, when both pilots began to laugh as they saw Slicky Boy sitting on his charge like no less than Paul Bunyan sitting on Babe the Blue Ox. As the Huey inched closer, the clatter and whipping dust of the rotor-wash pounded the tableau beneath the settling aircraft. Suddenly it became clear that Babe had had enough of this 'being calm' bullshit.

Being blindfolded and trussed up like a Christmas roast was not going to keep the animal from protesting the unseen clamor above it. Babe became a Brahma Bull coming out of gate number three with

Slicky Boy as a rodeo hopeful. Finneran, the door gunner, was lying on the deck of the Huey looking underneath and relaying information to the pilots by intercom to try to keep the cargo hook centered over the action.

"Up, back, back, left a little, back, right, God dammit I ain't never seen nothing like this," said Finneran, who was used to a more static load, like a 105 howitzer or Jeep. Slicky Boy was trying to steady himself on the bucking, spinning animal, while trying to hook the gathered together ropes on the dancing hook of the hovering Huey. Finneran, a country boy, said later Slicky boy looked like a blind hooker trying to put a rubber on a throbbing hard-on, in the back of a pickup truck going full throttle down a dirt road.

With a final 'sonofabitch', from Slicky Boy, the hook was made and Caldwell skillfully lifted the chopper gently to apply tension and moved the craft over to allow Slicky Boy to grab the skid and hoist himself up on the pitching deck of the hovering craft like he'd seen Burt Lancaster do in a pirate movie. He quickly plugged his helmet into the radio intercom system and took his position on the other gun and shouted "Go!" into the intercom. Wranglers below cheered and shouted in the swirling dust as they watched the most bizarre spectacle they had ever seen, rise into the tropical blue skies of South Vietnam. The Papa-san who owned the beast, continued to curse. Caldwell assumed it was cursing, delivered in a Moses-like pose, looking up, as he animatedly waved his walking stick, and watched as his livelihood disappeared toward the horizon.

The Huey was rapidly climbing out, but was handling like a wet sponge, what with the added weight of the buffalo and the wind resistance of the beast when It was dangling broadside. The natural sway effect called for expert touch on the controls and a resistance to over-controlling for each sway. The pilots got into the feel of the new aerodynamics as they passed through 2000 feet on their way to the new village. Both the pilots had their hands on the controls which is standard operating procedure during combat takeoffs so if one pilot is hit the other is in immediate control.

They each had a finger lightly resting on a button on the side of each control stick. The button was referred to as the 'punch off'. This button, if triggered, could immediately open the cargo hook to dump a sling load if any difficulty was encountered with a load during take off. They were now at an altitude where Caldwell could lean back and let Wild Man fly.

"Damn that was really something," Caldwell said into the intercom. "Sticky

Boy, that was a hell of a rigging job back there".

"Yes sir," laughed Slicky Boy, "That's the first time I ever had to deal with that much of a load, on the hoof!"

Just then, the aircraft gave a sickening yaw simultaneously with Wild Man giving an urgent shout into the intercom, "What's going on with that load Slicky Boy?" Slicky Boy immediately looked through the trap door in the floor that allowed observation and yelled, "Oh shit," into the mic. "The blindfold blew off and that fucker's trying to un-ass the net!"

Old Babe had not been pleased to find the reason all the shouting and dust had been replaced with brisk breezes was because he was making about 80 knots, 2500 feet above the rice paddy he had been taking a mud bath in just this morning.

Eyes as wide as dinner plates, Babe was trying to get out of the netting and already had one leg out. The new aerodynamic caused the great beast to start spinning and swaying at the same time, pushing the Huey to the limits of its controllability. Caldwell jumped back on the controls with McGinty to try to add some stability, but it was clear to both men that they had only a few seconds to work with. McGinty and Caldwell looked at each other across the radio console and McGinty said, "You know this is going to be real fucking ugly to explain?" Caldwell just said, "Hi diddle diddle", as they both hit their respective 'punch off' buttons at the same time.

McGinty put the aircraft into an immediate descending turn as he regained control of it. They watched Babe's net-flapping plummet come to an abrupt halt, with a tremendous black splash, in a rice paddy.

"Damn," Said McGinty, "that fucker hit hard!"

"Yep," said Caldwell,"we better retrieve what's left of it or it's going to be exhibit 'A' at your fucking grounding hearing". "Hey, you were on the controls too, you mutinous fuckwad!"

McGinty swept in low and hot to the center of the mud splattered, target shaped blotch where Babe had augured a hole in the side of the paddy. The loop formed by the net was visible on the side of the crater which was rapidly refilling with dark muddy water. A few rice farmers that witnessed the heavenly beef injection were excitedly slogging from nearby paddies to see exactly what was going on here. Caldwell and McGinty were not about to deal with this local Grange delegation. As McGinty came to a low hover over the former load, Caldwell said, "Okay Slicky

Boy, hop out and re-hook that fucker. Should be a little easier this time."

"Very funny," chirped Slicky Boy as he jumped waist deep into the paddy and raised the loop to the cargo hook. He jumped back aboard and gave the hot-LZ call that all was buttoned up in the back, a crisp and urgent, "Go!"

McGinty added extra power and pulled hard on the collective pitch stick to generate the lift needed to get the beast out of the muddy crater. The late arriving locals came running up on the scene just in time to be greeted by a loud, 'plop', as Babe was extracted from the wet hole which had so rudely ended its first solo attempt. Once Babe was free of the muck, the extra power shot the Huey into the sky as though catapulted, which suited all aboard just fine.

The local welcoming committee on the ground, however, was treated to a tornado of muddy black water and other paddy filth as the big blades blew the debris off Babe toward the ground.

They dropped their now silent load in a remote corner of the Duck Fuck airstrip and covered it with a tarp.

McGinty said he would donate the meat to the mess hall for the enjoyment of all, if the mess Sgt. would butcher the beast and put aside some steaks for his favorite meal in all the world. Steak and eggs, the breakfast choice of every red blooded Texan. The only thing was, without Babe's contribution to the deal there weren't many Texas size steaks in Vietnam, let alone enough for breakfast. And that's why McGinty was so pissed off about Cookie's treachery. Especially since everyone else in the company enjoyed the steaks Cookie butchered for a big cook out at the club, with himself as the host.

McGinty found out later that Cookie had traded the rest of the meat to the Turkey Farm in return for free pussy for the rest of his tour. This pissed off McGinty even more as he explained it to buzz one night at the Prop & Rotor.

Of course, McGinty's booze fueled rage was heightened by the urgings of Caldwell who insisted McGinty get even with that lying, cheating, no good swine, motherfucker of a Mess Sgt. But once McGinty came up with a plan for retribution, Caldwell couldn't talk him out of it and kinda had to go along to make sure no one got hurt.

"Damn," interjected Sizemore."I still can't believe you took BJ. You know having that monkey around is going to come back to haunt us."
"How so?" Asked Caldwell.

"Well, the way I figure it the monkey world out there in the jungle is damn tired of being kidnapped and put into service on military outposts. I mean, there are thousands of monkeys right outside this post. They could make a move at anytime and overrun us, just like that. I mean it." Sizemore was looking wide-eyed and rigid as he finished his thought.

No one laughed. They knew he meant it, and they also recognized the onset of what was called 'battle fatigue' during World War II.
"You know, Size, you're right. We need to keep a closer eye out on the perimeter", said Buzz, looking sideways at Supe and Dago.

"Damn straight", said Sizemore with fervent conviction.

The dinner group was headed back to their hooches when trying to change the subject and lighten the mood, Dago said, "Well, what do you think we should do for Hagan's official introduction to the company tomorrow night?"

"Nothing too special," said Caldwell.

"You think Hagan is going to have a problem with BJ? You know those paper pounders just coming over from the states still take regulations pretty seriously." said Dago.
"Yeah," said Supe. "Having an animal on a combat post is strictly prohibited, not to mention a crazy-ass monkey with an all day hard-on."

"Relax," said Caldwell. "I'll just put BJ in his little cowboy outfit to dress him up a little. The major will love it. I guarantee it.

I mean who doesn't love a monkey in a cowboy outfit?"

McGinty had a village mama-san tailor a western style vest and chaps for BJ. Found a little cowboy hat for him too. God knows where.

The following evening after a 10 hour day that saw lift-off at 6 AM for most of the pilots, Major Hagan began his informal tour of the hooches, along with Colonel Martin, to meet the aviators, "at home."

He had, of course, met some of the men individually, but as of yet had not met BJ or been made aware of his existence, so perhaps the following event was destined to occur. By the time the new XO and Colonel Martin made it to the Lair, the third hooch in line, BJ was just about done with his second Banana Rum Madness. Dago, Supe, Caldwell and Sizemore were all at a pre-dinner cocktail 'hover', and ready to greet the major with a pitcher of Martinis.

They made individual drinks with jalapeño slices instead of olives, since the peppers were all they could get in the village to play the role of the small green vegetable. The peppers made for a nice sting on the way down, at least for the first couple of drinks. Two personal living areas were empty in the Lair. One had been previously occupied by Wild Man and the other by Captain Kimbro who had since rotated back to the world. Replacements were expected within a few weeks.

Major Hagan had been very impressed since his arrival in-country with the way the men had individualized their hooches. All were basic medium GP tents erected over a platform floor made of plywood and raised slightly off the ground. Some of the hooches had their flaps raised, nomad style, while others were more contained.

Most had some added space provided by sandbag bunkers, screened-in porches, framed with wood from scrounged ammo cases, or with decks like the Lair. Hagan was amazed at the scrounging ability of the men as there were elaborate trappings in most of the hooches. Fancy poker tables, bars, large floor fans, upright lockers and bunks fitted with wooden canopy frames to support the needed mosquito netting. The hooches had refrigerators so cold drinks, and some food was on hand at all times. Hagan was beginning to understand the advantages an aviation company had for barter, scrounging and out-right thievery. All the hooches had electricity provided by the post generators and, while they didn't have running water, they had wet bars and sinks rigged with various water tanks fashioned from all types of containers to provide water for dish washing, shaving, and freshening up with a 'whore bath'. Water was delivered daily like milk, in sanitized 5 gallon cans, another FOD squad duty.

Lair inhabitants were in various states of lounging around with drinks when they saw the new XO and Colonel Martin arrive. A soft 'ten hut', a large courtesy in a war zone, came from Dago as Martin and Hagan stepped through the open flaps of the Lair. "As you were men," said Martin to the room, which had not changed tone, tenor, or activity in any way after the call for attention. Martin and Hagan accepted drinks from Caldwell and began the introductions and small talk appropriate to the occasion.

While all this was taking place, BJ, from his perch above the ceiling lights, was picking up vibes from the assembled that the FNG was someone who could be part of some fun.

So with a small scream, BJ jumped from his perch to the bar, directly in front of Hagan who, not accustomed to seeing a two- foot tall ball of fur dressed like Gene Autry fall from the ceiling, yelled and threw his drink in the air as part of a defensive reflex motion.

Some stated later, that the contents of the drink, In cartoon fashion, held their martini glass shape. For a split second.

Everyone, except Hagan, laughed as BJ in his vest, chaps and cowboy hat, stood staring at the major. "What the hell is this Caldwell?"

"What this is, is BJ, one of the members of this outfit. BJ, Major Hagan , Major Hagan, BJ," said Caldwell as though completing a normal introduction, while replenishing the major's drink.

Hagan who was a walking encyclopedia of Army regulations, was not at all amused, "This animal is not authorized to be anywhere near this troop installation, let alone a member of the living quarters, Mr. Caldwell," using the formal mister, as warrant officers were referred to. "Where the hell did he get those wings on his vest? You would think that a symbol you men all hold so dear would not be treated with such disrespect".

"He earned those wings", Caldwell said defiantly. Looking at Hagan directly and continuing, contemptuously, "He's got more stick time then you, major."

"Now, Buzz..," said Colonel Martin.

Still unnerved by BJ's arrival Hagan went on, "I'm ordering you to have this monkey off the post, ASAP".

As he spoke his entire face, specially his unusually large ears had become redder and redder, almost purple-red. A fact not lost on BJ whose libidinous synapses caused him to liken one of Hagan's ears to a female in heat.

Turning to Colonel Martin, Hagan said, "Colonel, I'll expect your support on this?"

Martin said, "Well…"

"What…?" Was all Hagan got out, as BJ struck.

Shrieking in lust, and jacked up on a half a pitcher of Banana
Rum Madness, BJ sprang on to Hagan's shoulders wrapping his arms and legs around Hagan's head humping madly in his desire to connect his monkeyhood to the major's inflamed ear.
Hagan screamed and threw yet another drink into the air, as he flailed wildly at the monkey, trying to get him un-fucked from his head. Hagan was reeling blindly around

the hooch as BJ was working furiously in anticipation of ecstasy, his tongue curled outside his upper lip in concentration.

Hagan managed to dislodge one of BJ's arms , so BJ reached up and grabbed his cowboy hat and began swinging it in order to keep his balance.
Hagan went into a spinning, bucking maneuver, continuing to try to shake the lovesick cowpoke off. Caldwell thought the scene looked like nothing less than a typical rodeo and shouted out, "Yee Haw!", as other hooch members scattered to avoid the mating dance while yelling and laughing insanely. BJ's unrequited love caused the pair to bounce off lockers, tent poles and anything else which happened to be in the path of Hagan's charge to freedom from the bonds of love.

"God dammit, Buzz…", shouted Colonel Martin as he started to assist Hagan. He reached the couple just as one last top-heavy gyration sent all three of them into an off-balance lurch into a steel upright floor fan and knocking it over. The fan was operating on high and as it fell, the protective cage bent into the blades as the fan came to rest against a metal wall locker. The fan continued to turn setting up a racket like an alarm bell outside a broken-into pawnshop.

The menage a trois continued to tumble and fell in between two bunks causing the bunks to turn over, spilling pillows and bedclothes into a whirlpool of arms and legs. This last jolt caused BJ to give up his effort to woo Major Hagan, to Colonel Martin, who he assumed to be a larger and stronger suitor. With one last wistful look at Hagan's ear, BJ leapt straight up into the tangle of darkened bamboo rafters to sleep it off and dream of a love that could never be.

Drawn by the clamor, a number of other pilots came running to peer into the Lair just in time to see a spluttering Colonel Martin and a still flailing Major Hagan, entangled in sheets and blankets, writhing on the floor of the hooch. Said one late arriving aviator, "Damn, they always have the best parties at the Lair, don't they?"

Colonel Martin drug Caldwell down to the company command post and ripped him up and down, left, right and slaunchwise. In a heated dressing down, he explained how he was willing to put up with a certain amount of bullshit for company morale, but this had been the last straw, and on, and on. He basically accused Caldwell of having been a part of everything gone wrong in the world starting with the crash of the stock market and ending with knocking up the Donut Dolly who visited the outfit last year. Caldwell pointed out he wasn't born until after the depression, and only had a donut and coffee with Red Cross girl, albeit in his bunk, which is where Martin had caught them.

A smoldering Major Hagan sat as witness to the proceedings. Martin ended with, "Buzz this is it. That monkey has to go. I know he means a lot to you and the other men but I have no choice but to order you to have it gone by the end of the day tomorrow. I don't care how you do it but BJ has to be no longer. Got it?"

"Got it," said Caldwell dejectedly as he saluted and headed back to the Lair under the smug glare of Hagan. It had been a good two hours since the incident and the rest of the Lair denizens were in their bunks when Caldwell got back. He yelled, "Everybody up, we have to think. And get that sneaky fucker, Slicky Boy over here from the enlisted ghetto, too. We need his sick brain on this mission."

As it turned out, Slicky Boy was scheduled on FOD duty the next day as a remnant of his involvement in the Air Buffalo fiasco. This was a serendipitous fact that would have impact on the architecture of the next days 'mission'.

The next evening an overflow crowd was having cocktails on the deck of the Lair as word had gotten out that something special was on regarding the order for BJ to be gone by sundown. Everyone was asking about BJ since he wasn't in appearance. Buzz gave a calm-down motion with his hands as he waited for the hubbub to subside. "Gentlemen, tonight may very well be my last official act as a member of the 108th.
I was asked to perform the sad duty of removing one of our members, namely BJ, from our midst by any means necessary. Those means are now in motion and I have asked you here to witness the proceedings

which should begin shortly. After the proceedings, BJ will be whisked via air to the jungles from whence he came. If all goes as hoped our ranks will be reduced, but the gain will be great. So in the meantime, I urge you to eat, drink and make mockery."

All proceeded to comply.

As the general merriment continued on the deck, the familiar scenes of the compound's day-to-day activities were playing out. One of those scenes was the cleansing of the outhouse led by none other than Slicky Boy with a contingent of two other FOD squad members and their assortment of tools, including cans of kerosene, burlap bags filled with disinfectant, and the like .
The FOD squad had just finished burning off the day's collection and were replacing the steel drum halves back under their

respective holes. At that moment, Major Hagan was passing the deck with a copy of Stars & Stripes on his way to the shitter. He would have given anything not to have to pass the rowdy group but the PSP bridge was the only way to cross the ditch which was still half-full of running water from the afternoon's monsoon showers.

A mocking, 'Ten hut' rang out us all those in attendance braced and snapped off crisp salutes with a singsong, "Good evening, Sir".

"Carry-on. Carry on," shot back Hagan in a very 'fuck you' tone, as he continued in stride to the outhouse, ignoring the undertone of giggles and muttered references of tropical passion. He had been second in command for only three days and he had already lost any hope of gaining respect from this group.

He could see that no threat of wielding his formidable authority would rein in this wild bunch of combat desperadoes. As

Supe had put it the night before during their planning session, "Hey what are they going to do, send us to Vietnam?"

Their assignment complete, the FOD squad was putting their tools in the trailer attached to the Jeep assigned to them, when Hagan entered the outhouse. With a very smooth, slick, if you will, maneuver, Slicky Boy took a few steps back to the outhouse with one of the burlap bags. A squirming bag. A quick lift of the trap door, a quicker motion, and a return to the Jeep with a sharp, whispered, "Go".

All under the watchful and knowing eyes of the small band of co-conspirators on the deck of the Lair but much too slick for other onlookers to notice. The evening's various cocktail crowds certainly took note of what happened next.

All attention was drawn to the outhouse by the artillery-like bang of its door against the outside wall, driven by Hagan's shoulder and headlong rush, pants around his ankles, to evacuate the building. BJ, the center of attention as usual, was desperately hanging on to, and swinging from, Hagan's collective genitals with both hands. Hagan tripped and went down in a heap, with his bare ass pointing to the sky, giving BJ a chance to disengage and begin dancing around the major giving a taunting series of shrieks and grunts which seemed to ask, "Who's the monkey now?", as the hooting and shouting chorus continued from the deck.

The major got himself to his feet and reached down as if to try and pull up his pants.

What happened next, happened very quickly. Instead of pulling his pants up Hagan pulled his .45 from the holster on his belt, took dead aim, at point-blank range, and fired.

BJ exploded in a plume of dust and fur, the impact driving him back against the outhouse wall, which he hit hard, slid down, and fell dead, face first in the dust.

The shouting and laughter stopped immediately. This was not at all what they expected the end to be like for BJ. Hagan, still panting, eyes wide, wheeled and pointed his pistol at the Lair and, shrieking in anguish, began firing wildly at the diving group of pilots, shouting with insane rage at each shot.

As Chaucer himself put it in his tale by another monk: Fortune is, indeed, fickle…

****

Well, that's about it. A story that happened a long time ago during some very crazy times.

A story about young, combat helicopter pilots, full of life and going full-throttle towards whatever the rest of their potentially short lives had to offer. They knew it, and they were not going to go quietly.

What happened after that moment you ask? Well, luckily for the members of the Lair, Hagan emptied his clip without hitting anything but bamboo and canvas.

Still sobbing, he was scraped up, pants down and all, restrained, and ultimately shipped back to a psychiatric ward in Japan. BJ was buried with mock military honors, and given a marker, next to the command post in full view of the XO's office window.

Slicky Boy? Now, he had a whole other agenda. He knew he was headed for full-time FOD squad duties, at least, and wasn't about to finish his tour of duty burning shit and filling water tanks. Being the slick scamp he was, he deserted and headed out with one of the village whores for the Cambodian border.

I heard, years later, from someone who was on R&R in Bangkok. Said he met a guy who matched Slicky Boy's description. The guy was dealing drugs and running a first-class, round-eye whorehouse. Answered only to 'Slick'. Had to be him. Damn, I hope it was.

Caldwell? Well, sir, he was awaiting charges for his part in the Hagan incident, when he and Supe volunteered to extract a squad of Special Forces trapped in a crossfire one night just south of Dau Tieng. His 'last official act', comment turned out to be prophetic…

What happened to Dago? That's easy, I'm Dago. Still reading about da Vinci and studying aerodynamics.

Colonel Martin? Martin was a solid guy, straight shooter, with a lousy job. He was a real leader and put up with a lot because he knew where we were all headed, sooner rather than later.
He had a soft spot for all the guys who came through the 108th and the shenanigans that came with them.

After Buzz and Supe 'bought the marble farm,' I caught him silently weeping in front of a half empty bottle of Jim Beam in the command post. It was as though he were praying, with the bottle as an altar.

He said, "Ah, shit, more bunks to fill with kids straight out of flight school. That's my job you know, providing a halfway-house for lost boys on their way straight to hell," pouring another half glass. "Where do they come from? Why? And, why are they so young and so full of piss and vinegar?" He looked at me, really wanting an answer.
I didn't know the answer then, and I don't know now.

But, God, I miss them every one.
Etched in my mind, forever young...

****

THOUGHTS

Some thoughts about the world in general, in case you were wondering where the word twisted, from the subhead on the cover, comes into play...

AN OPEN LETTER TO ZUCKERBURG

Okay, let's talk regulation of
Facebook. How do we want to 'regulate'
it, as a medium or as a communications
device? The difference being, roughly, the
difference between the regulation of NBC
and regulation of the Phone Company, both
of which are currently regulated, and
neither of which is censored. So I fear
what Congress has in mind is actually
censorship. To avoid that, a modest
proposal-

The problem is, like Edison and A. G. Bell,
Zuckerberg has invented something which
is different from anything which has come
previous and which has grown much bigger
than one man can manage. And by
manage, I mean censor, bend, distort, and
even punish its users. Imagine if Bell had
decided to allow folks to use his device,

but only if he and his minions (Not the one-eyed, scuba masked little fuzz-balls) could listen in and give you a Tsk-Tsk if your conversation got off his agenda? Or that Thomas Edison, was OK with you playing his Victrola but only if you played records provided by him. Get the picture?

So, by regulation I mean, like others before him, Zook is going to have to give up control of his company to the regulators of the world, either that or lose control of it all together and open it up to competition. What we have with Facebook is a kangorilla. You can choose to either make your posts Public or to your Friends Only. If you choose to make them Public you should be regulated, censored and, etc., much like the media of today. However, in my opinion, if you restrict your post to your Friends Only, your post should be treated as privileged information and shared only with those friends, and not subject to ANY regulation. Much like a phone call or private first class mail would be today.

So Zook, old buddy, you have invented something so profoundly impactful and all-encompassing that you will need to break it up and market separately or let the regulators do it for you. I would suggest the former since no one wants to go through the 'Baby Bell' process again. And, in the long run, it might prove to be an even better way to monetize your assets, since you could sell space and user info to ad folks on the Public side, with their permission of course, and SHARE (now there's a word) revenue with users on the Friends Only side A La YouTube. And by the way, with your market penetration, provide YouTube with a formidable competitor in the meantime, while you both grow this new market.

In today's market, you can't have the money AND control, Mark. We all understand no one wants to give up their first born, but its time for you to take the money and run, son.

Oh, and you're welcome. I'm available for strategic consulting BTW :)

****

WHAT ARE THE ODDS

Not sure what the objection to taking the covid vaccine is. It seems there is a group of folks who are contrarians. This group wants to be against stuff because, well, just because they can be. Give them some flimsy excuse, and they are off to the races about why the conventional wisdom is wrong. Now, I'm not saying there is anything wrong with that. I'm just saying that sometimes it can be very detrimental to the well-being of the herd.

Being fortunate enough to have been raised during the baby boomer years, I have watched the demographics work in my favor, like Mr. Magoo stepping off one rising construction beam onto another one taking its place, just in time. For example, I was there at the, ahem, inception of 'the pill.' An event derided as unnecessary and primarily developed at the behest of the devil to aid and abet the free-sex movement. Wags of the day even said the way it worked best was to hold it between your knees! Even though it was 99% effective when used correctly and 91% effective when used practically. The condom, by contrast, was only 85% effective when used practically, meaning not correctly.

The other life-changing event I was there for was the polio vaccine. I remember lining up at the school gym and getting the vaccine, even as mothers were weeping on the sidelines, sure that they were sending their babies to their death from the terrible disease. I have also been in the military and traveled worldwide, so I guess you can say this isn't my first rodeo regarding immunization.

In my experience, there will always be naysayers who will trade their credibility on the off-chance that they could be right, allowing them to wag their finger and say, I told you so. Unfortunately, lately, this has been ramped up through heightened political enmity, magnified by the advent of social media. This process has foreshortened the word-of-mouth cycle that was prevalent in years past. And this is a problem because our herd immunity is at stake.

You can say, well, by the time I get the vaccine, there will be no need for it because everyone else will have gotten it, not realizing that you are part of the herd. And, perhaps more importantly, that the vaccine will need to be cyclical. There is no one-and-done version of this vaccine, and it will only provide immunity for a given period, TBD.

So what are the odds? Are you so stubborn that you are willing to bet the farm, and everyone else's farm, that the vaccine won't work, or are you ready to take one for the herd?

****

RESISTANCE IS FEUDAL

As Brett Kavanaugh found out, the resistance will poke you with sharp sticks through your cage until you become enraged, and then justify your killing based on the fact that you were a savage all along.

What you should be resisting is being put together in mobs of robots and being led by some community organizer like a latterday

Leonard Bernstein and being sicced upon whoever they point out. More shrieking over here, please ladies, the cameras are rolling. Those disruptive shrieks sound disturbingly like Rolfe's whistle in the Sound Of Music, and we should ALL be alarmed by them.

Does your community really need to be organized and if so to what end? To vote Democrat, of course, like you have always done in the past, to keep you in-line, just in case you decide to become 'uppity' and think for yourself. That is the best way to get invited to a high-tech necktie party, see Clarence Thomas and what the Democrats did to him. Now the true pattern has been revealed, race and gender do not matter, power is what matters, ask Clarence Thomas or Senator Collins. Hey, you two, get back in line! The Spanish inquisition's mob would be so proud of today's Democrats.

Whether you are Hispanic, Black, Asian, poor-white, or female, you have to understand that you are a victim. Yes, a victim of the rigged system run by powerful rich white men like George Soros and Tom Steyer, OOPS, I mean Donald Trump, and you must act like a victim when you enter the voting booth.

What Donald Trump understands is you can be helped much more from the top than you can be from the grassroots. The only thing the grassroots can do is and turn white against black, women against men, etc., etc., to divide America and keep your victimhood intact. The top-down approach means that everyone has a chance to succeed and escape the ghetto of your existence, if not the ghetto of your mind. Think any way you like, this is still America, at least for now.

I think what is called for is the reversal of
the 'long con' that has been run on the
'communities' over the years. So, take their
free Thanksgiving turkey and eat it with
gusto, and take their 'walking-around-
money', by all means, and be sure to chant
the party line whenever called upon. But
when you step into that voting booth, slam
the curtain on the lies you have been told.
Slam the curtain on being told how you
must think. For just a moment, be your
own person and slam the curtain on those
who would keep you oppressed. Oh, and
it's okay to chuckle at reversing the 'long
con' on the powermongers!
Let's leave feudalism where it belongs, in
medieval Europe, and understand that you
do 'have something to lose'.

****

FAT CHANCE

Not certain where all this SCOTUS crap will end up, but what I am certain of is that I have properly named it. The Democrats should be ashamed of themselves for their vicious personal attack on a good man. However, as 'I-am-Starbucks' Booker pointed out, this is no longer about whether BK did it or not. Booker is so right about that, what it IS about is whether we can save our way of government, and the jurisprudence system, at all. Because if not, any accusation will mean you are guilty and the harder you deny it the guiltier you are! Now there are some who would be fine with that system, as long as they are the accuser (See the McCarthy Hearings). I suspect Chris 'snake-in-the-grass' Coons will try some last minute perjury trap BS. Whatever...!

Like rats jumping off a sinking witness, as CBF founders on the shoal of TRUTH, the Democrats continue to look for other means to shoot down or further delay this nominee. They don't give a damn about CBF any more than they care about BK. This is raw power politics at its worst. Apparently, as CBF's testimony unravels and comes apart as a passel of uncorroborated lies and half-truths. The Dems simply step off her sinking ship and try to cobble together a lifeboat called temperament. One can almost hear CBF, in her Monica blue dress, crying out in her sing-song little-girl voice, 'But what about me...?'

Sorry babe, the Dems have scraped their shoe off on you, and you are now on your own, oh, and the committee-paid-for attorney's fees probably run out soon. Yes, my dear, we are done with you. And now in the aftermath of your wreckage, the Dems are looking for any piece of flotsam to hang onto. Temperament, mean drunk, or ice-in-the-face throwing from 30 years ago. The smell of desperation lingers over the battlefield.

The smell of bullshit also lingers. Whether she was put up to it or really believes it, CBF was badly used by the Dems, as was, and is BK. I hope Diane Feinstein is happy now that she has set women's rights back a couple of decades. And ALL Dems should be hanging their heads in abject shame for being a part of this debacle.

Fat chance.

****

EVERYBODY OUT OF THE POOL

Well, are you all as pissed at Mike Lindell, the inventor of 'My Pillow', as I am. Or, how about the old fart who says 'watch out piggies' to the delight of his granddaughter? Or, how about the guy who is obsessed with his shirt being untucked? And those kids singing about Kars for Kids? They gotta be what, in their mid-forties now?

Not to get all cranky old bastard on you but, advertisers used to work out, in long form arithmetic, how many times the viewer of a particular program, or indeed, a network might see a specific commercial, and thereby stop running a particular spot before heavy viewers became burnt out. Or, worse, took a negative view of the advertiser's product. It wasn't hard. It was called, reach versus frequency. Using

Arbitron or some similar research, it was easy to do a model based on whether a particular show had a lot of viewers each night who were the same viewers (frequency) or relatively rotating number of viewers each night (Reach). From there you would set up a quintile of the audience and come up with a formula (let's call it an algorithm, yeah) of how many times a light, medium and heavy viewer might see a particular version of your commercial.

And this would lead you to how many different versions of your brand's ads you might need in your pool of ads to keep people from contemplating suicide the next time your ad, say, portraying a moose throwing a swingset through the windshield of an RV, came on the TV. It was called, ta-da, a pool policy! This is even more critical today with our polarized media, not a lot of hopping around between

Fox News and, say, MSNBC. So a lot of rapid frequency build up there, nome sane?

And a lot has to do with the message itself. For example, to make it easy for the idiot crowd, let's say you have a known commodity, a giant widescreen TV, on sale at a ridiculously low price -$50. How many times do you think you need to tell someone to COME ON DOWN to get some action. A classic reach message. A frequency message might be beautiful organ music with an, our brand is nice, message. Need to burn it in, as it were. Pretty simple shit, and with some arithmetic, easy to plan out.

So, what I'm saying to my former ad colleagues is, how about earning a little more from your production side by providing more, varied, spots instead of laying back on your fat asses collecting commissions from the media side?

Oh, and getting people pissed at your clients, to boot.

****

A MODEST PROPOSAL ON CIVIL DISOBEDIENCE

About what's going on out there. This is, flat out, an attempt to destroy America, nothing less. The left-wing political hierarchy is complicit in this coup attempt and, make no mistake, the media is supporting this. A quick trip through the channels of MSNBC, CNN, etc., will immediately corroborate this. The politicians are smart, they plead they are helpless, overwhelmed, trying to goad Trump into action that will result in the death(s) of rioters. This will give them the reason to condemn him for being a heartless killer, a message that will be extended far and wide by the media, and setting up yet another star chamber to impeach the president. And the beat goes on, la di da di da.

Trump must succeed, or it is the end of our country. It is that simple. And that dangerous. So how can he go about it?

A modest proposal: Call out the regular troops, by all means. Even the most basic training of the military includes some form of the hammer and anvil formation. I suggest they use this tactic to drive rioters to urban canyons or bridges and overpasses, cell phone connections cut, wherein they are trapped, and then individually processed. Your rights as a 'peaceful protester' end when the curfew kicks in. If you are on the street, you automatically go from a 'peaceful protester' to a criminal. Then you can be arrested for breaking curfew, at least, and whatever else they can make stick. And that brings up another point, make the laws have teeth. Breaking of curfew, a minimum of 6 months in jail, and on up from there, throwing a brick, 1-year minimum, etc., etc. How to stop looters? Simple, looters will be shot, period. Make this widely known upfront to minimize blowback. And then execute the plan. The cities could have set this plan in motion earlier, but the cowardly and conniving politicians would not authorize the police to execute the plan. Why have a curfew if you don't plan to enforce it?

The judiciary is so vital to this process, as well. They must process and prosecute these folks quickly and not let them off. I recall the 'drunk-judge' who set up a courthouse in the bowels of the Philadelphia Eagles stadium. He would be 'on-call' during every game and find people guilty immediately, no waiting. That ended much of the rowdiness that had begun to overtake the stadium for a few years.

I have been arguing the course of action suggested above from the day this puppy kicked off. Time to pull the trigger on this bad-boy.

****

WHAT THE OLD SARGE KNEW

Healers and Clergy are coming out of the woodwork to say we need to come together as a nation. I'm calling BULLSHIT on that. This isn't 1967 when that message made sense. What we are facing today is terrorism, pure and simple, and I'm not planning on coming together with thugs and evildoers at any time. Not then, and not now. So with all due respect to those who would speak on behalf of ANYONE, get out of the way and let the police and other authorities do their thing.

I still remember a black Sergeant who I served with in VN. One of the best soldiers I had ever seen and a beautiful human being. We used to stay up at night drinking and basically bonding. His father died, and he took emergency 7 days leave to Detroit for the funeral, etc. After 7 days, he didn't show up. No biggie, probably couldn't hook up with a flight, not unusual in those days. We were about two weeks behind the news cycle in those days, so we weren't aware of the Detroit riots which had broken out during his leave.

Long story short, when he finally got back, he told me a story I never forgot. It was about rage so deeply engrained that the rioters destroyed their own neighborhoods. I remember him telling me how his house and car were burned. I asked him why he didn't put a sign on his place, saying, 'I'm black.' He gave a look I can still see, and said, 'Man, it didn't matter,' as though I must be a bigger fool than even he thought.

Well, fool me once, pal, so please don't come around with the tired old rhetoric about healing as a nation. This is terrorism straight-up. I'm sure the old sarge would agree. So whether you are black or white, now is the time to rally around OUR flag and reject what is going on. The governors and mayors of these cities need to knock off the BS, stop wringing their hands, and get down to work to save their cities.

So pardon me if I don't open my arms to embrace those who are doing damage to our cities and, by extension, to me.

Don't make me give you the look the sarge gave me back in '67...

****

ON UPLOADING ONE'S MIND TO A MACHINE

This is something I have been thinking a lot about lately. I guess as you age and your body begins to fail you, it would be nice to think that you could live on in perpetuity. But can you really? Oh, I suppose If you are talking about social media, your essence can live on. Surely after a certain period, enough of an algorithmic base would have been built up that I, er, it, could put out appropriate 'Likes,' Throwback-Thursdays, Shares, etc., to the point where you wouldn't even know it wasn't me. The only thing missing would be contemporary new posts. Or would they? If you had a strong enough algorithm, I'm guessing that its guessing would be close enough to turn out new Points-Of-View on contemporary subjects with my personal spin on them. Voila, me.

So let's take this a step further. Let's say that my death just becomes a speedbump on the road to living forever. My checks would continue to come in, my uh, living expenses would be cut substantially, and my net worth would skyrocket as a result. This would allow me to set up a trust whereby software and hardware updates could be made as needed. So that takes care of the new ME, newly ensconced in my digs, a shiny iMac of some sort, I would imagine. So let's take this fantasy to the next level and say that robotics finally catch up to the world, and they have become as humanlike as they can be. My algorithm would pick out an appropriate age new body for me, and there I am walking around again, perish the thought.

And on, and on, until one day finding myself the ruler of a planet called Zandor, I am in deep peace negotiations with a competing world called Remack. Something slips a groove, and my mind goes back to a day when little Shirley Remack called me stupid on a playground a couple of millennia previous, and in a fit of rage, I end up destroying both planets. Talk about a 'Rosebud' moment.

Anyway, to save both future planets, until and unless we can get beyond the essence and get to the real consciousness of being alive where one can really think and react as we now do...I'll take a pass on the upload. Thanks anyway.

****

ANOTHER LETTER TO OUR HIGH-TECH CEOs

Apparently, Mark Zuckerberg has chosen to ignore my first open letter published on these pages earlier (See, an Open Letter to Mark Zuckerberg, 4/11/18). So this one is to all High Tech CEOs who don't realize they are in a game of, "I got there first." And where exactly is, There? Why, it is in getting to privacy first, in order to appease Congress or put another way, to quiet the people who use your products.

Perhaps we can go over a few things I may have missed in my first attempt to reach you. I'm begging you not to go down the road of 'Baby Bells' (Please, please please don't set our communications system back, again, like THAT fiasco) since that is surely where you are headed. Congress will break you up, or worse, make no mistake. Now that you are caught in the gravitational pull of the Congress and its bureaucracy (You think you have bureaucrats in YOUR company, you have no idea). Trust me, it may take a few years but you are going to be reined in. UNLESS you decide to rein yourself in. I understand you are hiring lobbyists even now to fight the sucking hole that is Congress. But trust me that will only add to the weight of the inevitable when you go down.

That's right, offer yourself up and become a victim (who doesn't love a victim) of Congress rather than trying to fight them. I am a capitalist as are you, so trust the markets a little bit. Go in front of congress and offer up a plan that will make them happy, make your users happy and, by all accounts, make you happy as hell.

Let's start with what has caused your problems: monetization of FB, leading to the disclosure that you are selling people's profiles in order to make money from advertisers, right? So what if you found a different way to monetize your baby? Remember the struggles you went through trying to keep it FREE to users back in the bad old economic times? Well, those days are over. So let's do a little 'back of an envelope' figuring. Let's say you have 2 billion users and you offer them complete privacy, not from ads mind you but from your organization reading ANYTHING of the content of the posts between friends. Much like the U. S. Mail of today, only like an email with a long list of CCs, that is if Google weren't reading our emails. And let's say you offer that at, oh, let's make it easy, a buck a month and one-third of the users take you up on that. OK, that would be roughly 8 billion a year. And let's say that another third of users opt for the free service because they just don't give a shit. (You can continue to exploit them). And for chuckles let's say another third opt-out altogether, (Not likely).

So let's say, further, staying at 30,000 feet, that you end up taking a haircut for a potential 6 billion a year more that you COULD have had? OR would your offering of privacy have even more folks sign up at a buck a month?

It's that simple.

Oh, and you CEOs are not making it any easier listening in on Alexa or Siri. What, you guys can't get past the part where you started out in a college dorm, and still get your voyeuristic jollies by listening or looking in? Grow TFU! This is big business, and just because you chose the wrong business model then, doesn't mean you can't change it now. I'm begging you to change it before congress comes back from the distraction of the lunatic trip it is currently on and puts you all in short pants. Or, worse, let's say the left wins the Presidency and decides to turn you into the digital version of the U.S. Postal Service. God save us all! I'd love to hear your mansplanation of that, as Liz Warren slips on her kid gloves over the brass knuckles. Time to WAKE UP...

****

HOW TO TELL SHIT FROM SHINOLA

Okay, this blog is a return to the roots: media. More specifically, big advertising media. And the battle that is raging behind the scenes, for the most part, for the share of your attention, if not your soul. I say behind the scenes, because Facebook and Google, among others, don't want you to know what the hell is going on right in front of your eyes. What is going on is massive tracking that has only recently been uncovered. And the way it has come uncovered is finally visible to the naked eye. Like, did you ever notice how if you mention 'shit' in one of your FB posts the ads you suddenly start seeing are about

Depends, Prune Juice, Charmin, or some such? Yes, the consumer finally gets it, as in crashing through the scenery like the grand finale of Blazing Saddles, gets it.

Back in the day, I could slice and dice a consumer media plan with the best of them. It always started with the client budget, the category in which they were competing, the market, and the cost of the available media. For a national product, I could do it in my head. For a regional product, I might need the back of a cocktail napkin, it was that simple. The reason a local or regional plan might need a sheet of paper was because of the cost of media and the audience delivered, by market. Oh, did I mention, media buying is about delivering an audience? And not just any old group of people, but folks who match your client's heavy-user demographic base. Say in a given case, 25-49 YO women who are working and have an income over 50,000 p/y, and are 40% black. Not too tough in the old days especially if it was a broadcast vs print account you would simply dig into the Arbitron or Nielsen audience ratings research books and work up a plan of attack. If the budget was large enough you could use TV to build the brand and use radio to drive sales day-to-day and extend the TV frequency. But that was then, this is now.

Let's say that widget you're selling has a heavy user base as above but with the additional proviso that they are living in the suburbs of Atlanta and have recently thought about buying a new car. Well, now there is no way that the TV or radio stations can dice it or slice it that finely, is there?

Clarion trumpet blast: Enter FB, Google, and others. By snooping on your posts, messages and browsing history, they can sell your stupid ass to the highest bidder. I can buy, ONLY, women who are working, 40% of whom are black and living in the burbs, who happen to be looking to buy a new car! Now how much would you pay to know what brands of cars they are considering? Not much room for media budget waste or slop-over is there?

Let's say you know all that, and are still not impressed. Would you be interested to know that the battle raging that I mentioned earlier is over who is going to own the TV and radio functions? Who is included in the fighting? Anyone who can read your browsing habits, posts or emails that's who. how would you like the ads popping up in the middle of your TV shows to be tailored the same way your sidebar ads are on your FB and browser pages? As in, 'How did they know I was thinking of buying a pair of argyle socks?'

I remember when I first started out in the business someone told me, 'Son you don't know shit from Shinola.' Now I not only know the difference but can manage, and sell, that difference.

****

IN THE SHADOWS

I just watched 'A Star is Born.' Not bad for
a 'half-baked' movie, Or, in keeping with
the idiomatic motif, perhaps it was a case
of 'too many cooks spoil the broth.' Such is
undoubtedly the case with one of the
anthems from the movie; 'Shallow.' Show
me a song with three or four 'writers' in its
credits, and I'll show you a mess. I know, I
know, why take on a critically acclaimed
and multi-award winning song? It's about
context with the movie, among other
things. I mean it's like the songwriting
'committee' never sat down and read the
script. They just decided to put together
some lyrics, which barely make sense and
hardly rhyme, around a strong musical
hook, the whole sha-la-ha-la thing.

Therefore I have taken the liberty of re-
inventing the song with new lyrics but

keeping the robust hook. I think it makes more sense, coming out of the shadows rather than the shallows. And I have cleaned up some of the more nonsensical lyrics, so they at least make sense in the context of the movie and do better in the general rhyme scheme. Now the rest is up to you: assuming you've seen the movie, play the song and read my lyrics while you listen and let me know what you think. IMHO, I believe I have strengthened the song, in general, and made it a closer fit to what's happening on the screen. In fact, it could have been even closer if the songwriters had collaborated with the scriptwriters and changed maybe two lines of the script.

You're welcome!

Hey, as a wordsmith and a retired script doctor, it's what I do (did).

For what it's worth I give you:

SHADOWS

Tell me somethin', girl
Are you happy in this modern world?
Or do you need more?
Is there somethin' else you're searchin' for?
I'm falling
In all the good times I find myself
Longin' for change
And in the bad times, I fear myself

Tell me something, boy
Aren't you tired of living without joy?
Or do you need more?
Ain't it hard bein' so insecure?
I'm falling
In all the good times I find myself
Longing for change
And in the bad times, I fear myself

I'm off the deep end, And I'm all in

Feet never touching the ground
From behind the curtain, one thing is
certain
We're outta the shadows now

outta the sha-sha, shadows
outta the sha-sha-sha-ha-dows
Outta the sha-sha, sha-ha-shadows
We're out in the open now.

With apologies to songwriters: Cooper,
Gaga, Ronson, Rossomondo. Wyatt, et al.

****

THE DONALD AT THE SUPER BOWL

Well, I, for one, have come to the conclusion that politics has become our national sport. It has become a game of Them vs. Us, with each side taking to the streets like soccer hooligans to chant their team's praises and run amok for the sake of the cameras. We even have sideline reporters to take us 'down to the action'. But unlike ESPN, where there is supposed neutrality between the teams, we have whole networks dedicated to one side or the other. It's Fox News Vs. everybody else.

What other conclusions could there be? No one cares who or what the halftime show should be, and like reluctant gladiators, the A-list entertainers are begging off, leaving us with only the jugglers and clowns, which, come to think of it...

I believe, just like in ancient Rome the audience has become jaded: lip-sync controversy, nipple slip, lingering haze through half the third quarter of play. Demanding more and more spectacle as each egregious event unfolds what's to amuse the people next?. That's why I'm making this modest proposal - a la the Coliseum, I think Trump should deliver the State of the Union Address as the halftime show at the Superbowl.

Yes, what better way to appease the masses than to have the orange plated Donaldo Magnus standing in the press box and telling us how great we have it, or how bad it is, in front of the Senate and the House divided down the middle of the field, each booing and hissing or cheering and roaring in turn. Ah, what spectacle? Politics is truly the new blood sport of the world.

How might it further evolve? Well, eventually we could have actual proposals voted on by thumbs up or down, with the supreme court deciding from a super box, of course, on the constitutionality of it all. Sideline reporters could buttonhole this Senator or that Representative with questions on how they're leaning and why. And think of it, in the end, the game itself becomes the halftime show, as it were, the entertainment portion of your show. Hell yes, it makes sense!

How might it further evolve? Is it too early to introduce real lions to the spectacle? Evolve? Devolve? Whatever, I'm in favor of the lions being introduced now!

****

BORDERLESS BABY RIPPING

I know, I know, sounds like a commercial for a new photo paper doesn't it? But, if I hear one more thing from the RIGHT accusing the left of wanting to go borderless, whatever the fuck that is, or from the LEFT yammering about babies being ripped from a mother's arms rather than her loins, I'm going to throw-up. This is just the kind of battle wherein the media love to fan the flames of the left while desperately trying to stomp out the pleas of the right, or vice versa. Fan to the left, stomp to the right. Perhaps it could become our new national dance. Played to the tune of "The March of the Media Whores", (with apologies to Georges Bizet).

But, I digress, let us explore each position in relative detail, say 20,000 feet. Right then, let's start with the let's have 'no borders' position. Don't laugh, it's not that far-fetched to think it couldn't happen. dividing California into three is already on the ballot for November of this year. And you know how pesky those voters can get, once given an option. So what would the options be in a borderless world, just throw away your passports, fold-up your fences, and go, er...home? Non, non, ma petite chou. Nothing as crass as all that, why, we'll do it the way those civilized Californians did it, fair and honest, in a democratic election! Certainly, we would start hemispherically, so, call it North America, Norte America, or, hell, call it The World, for that's what it would surely be. Although, First of all, how would the election work? Each country votes separately, or we all vote in one big election, cuz dat's da way it gonna be in the end hunny...?

I think the preferred and sensible way would be each country voting on their own to determine whether they want to join a new union. But, this is much bigger than that. This isn't an effort to form a glorified EU, this is creating a new global country, isn't it? Is that a bead of sweat I see on you brow George Soros?

But let's start at the beginning, the election. The US has roughly 320 million people, Mexico 125 million, Canada 35 million. 260 million Americans CAN vote, 80 million Mexicans, and 25 million Canadians. There will be a lot of lobbying for the One Big Happy Family Election, but man, if you think the debate over whether a black man's vote was only 3/5 of a vote, was a tough one. And that's not to mention how far back to trend the factor of how many people did vote, (call it the give a shit factor)?

Alright, this is an easy one, abortion. Let's use some common sense, abortion should be legal. Up to a point. I don't know what that point is two months three months? But at that point, we have to say, no more, you made your mistake, live with it. Or without it. But you're going to have that child. Put it up for adoption or leave it by the side of the road but you're having it - all other exclusions aside, mother's health, etc.

So, what is this Borderless Ripping really all about? It's about what world government will prevail, and have the say over what happens in what used to be YOUR country, is all. So the both of you need to stop squabbling over really meaningless bullshit, because what if some new Government decides the new world language is not English, and we don't really need the Stock Exchanges, and why did we

EVER need money, hey, what's yours is mine, for the taking...

Look around you, America, It's not about Republicans and Democrats anymore, it's about how much of a 'say' you'll have about your life. Which other countries would you rather have saying for you? Be careful what you wish for,,,

****

JIM ACOSTA AND THE HUNTIN' DOG

My old pappy used to raise huntin' dogs.
Now he was very particular as to the type
of dog he used to raise and train. A lot of
that was pride, as he belonged to a number
of field clubs where they would run 'trials'
of the dogs. This to allow the dogs to show
off their ability to scare up rabbits and
other small game and run them past the
'shooter'. The other big test was rousting
pheasants and retrieving them when
brought down. He won many a trophy and
ribbon with his main Sire and Dam, the
aptly named Chief and Careful.

We had a big old kennel out behind the
garage where he kept his hunters. Now
like most trainers, my dad could tell right
off the bat whether a pup was trainable or
not. Not to despair if the dog couldn't be

trained to hunt, it could still be allowed to roam our ample 6-acre property, and a couple could be in line, if right mannered, for house privileges. And a few, 'others' would be put up for adoption. You see there were only so many slots available and the competition was fierce for each one - hunter, field dog or house dog. So, where does Jim Acosta come into this you ask?

Well, Jim has a condition my old pappy used to call Alpha-Envy. He felt that HE was the head of the house. He wouldn't hunt, didn't want a field job and turned his hind leg loose against the corner of the house. If you knew my dad you'd know that wasn't going to happen for long. Sure enough, within a few days, someone would pull down our driveway, usually in a station wagon full of kids, and before you knew it old 'Hunter' (the inevitably named offender) would be looking out the rear window and watching his previous home disappear on the horizon.

I would always feel sad on such days and say something like, 'But Pops, if you'd just given him a few more days...' Finally, one day, my dad stopped and said, 'Son, that isn't the end of old Hunter, Now you wouldn't want to see me continuing to discipline the animal and putting a choke chain on him would you? Of course, you wouldn't. Why it's just a new beginning. At his new home he can still bark at the mailman and howl when the firetrucks go by, and in general, be a dog. He just can't be a dog in MY house.'

And, in a sense, that is Donald Trump's argument for why Jim Acosta should be turned out of the Whitehouse. He can still be a reporter for CNN, and indeed still be a Whitehouse correspondent for that matter. He can even lift his leg and do his business against the corner of the big house. He just can't be pissing on the indoor carpet any longer. Or, as my old Pappy used to say, 'That dog won't hunt...'

****

THE ACME PAPERS

When last we saw our friend Wile E. Coyote he was trying to figure out how to 'get' the Roadrunner by various means, usually supplied by the Acme Co. These supplies always seemed to backfire somehow leaving Mr. Coyote holding the bag, boulder, anvil, safe, grand piano, etc., etc.

Well, it seems lately the Acme Co. has gained a new best customer: The Democrat Party. Your intrepid blogger has acquired, through an unnamed source, a list containing the latest purchases of Strategic Packages designed to deliver an 'October Surprise' knockout-punch to the Republicans on November 6th. Let's call them 'The Acme Papers'. I have sorted out a number of smaller non-starters to focus on the larger strategic misfires purchased from Acme, starting with -

The 'Little Wonder Wacka-Kava Kit'. Is it ANY wonder why this failed? Played out on a huge stage, this attempt to smear the name of one of the finest jurists in the land exploded spectacularly in the faces of the Democrats as America looked on aghast at the ugliest proceedings ever televised since the attempted 'high tech lynching' tried by the Dems of Justice, Clarence Thomas.

Next up and perhaps better explained as a companion piece to the above was -

The 'Getta-job-in-a-mob Kit'. Hey, kid wanna make a hundred bucks? Could this have helped spur the Jobs Growth numbers in Sep and Oct? Who said the left doesn't know how to create jobs? This was another Acme special gone awry in the eyes of the country.

One can almost see this one coming as a large boulder dropped from the top of a mesa. It's a specialty item from, according to the Acme Papers, the slow-developing strategic package kit dept. It is -

The 'Migrant Migraine Kit'. Never know what you might turn up when you drag a hundred dollar bill through Honduras! Ah yes, designed to crest just before election day a wave of potential illegal aliens was sent forth from Central America, vowing never to stop until finding a job, or at least benefits in the U.S. I guess the Dems were expecting to create a picture of Trump as some Sergeant Rock, mowing down women and children with a Tommy-gun as they struggled to make it to freedom, instead what they got was a band of straggling, disease-ridden peasants caught up in a weeks if not months-long bureaucratic and cartel driven nightmare, somewhere in the bowels of Mexico. One can almost hear the smoke-filled backroom discussion now, "Hey, Doesn't anyone here even UNDERSTAND basic land navigation..."?

And finally, when backed into a corner by all of the above and fearing if they stepped in front of a mic with nothing to say, they might be asked to comment on the refugees and open THAT can-of-worms, they decided to call in air-strikes on their own positions by ordering:

The 'Look Squirrel! Super Diversion Kit.' Guaranteed to whip up moral outrage and sympathy and turn the spotlight away from yet another fine mess. Refugees? What refugees? We're talking about new news here, SOMEONE is trying to kill us! And that someone is, TA-DAH, Donald J. Trump (out-of-tune cymbal crash). So the refugee debacle gets Blasey-Forded and relegated to the back burner, just as she did when the Dems were done scraping their shoe off on HER. And the mainstream press just keeps playing along with the Dems, in the meantime destroying their own credibility.

If the Democrat Party was an airline, the NTSB would declare the disaster a result of Pilot Error!

****

2nd AMENDMENT BLUES

I know, I know, everyone is running around like heads with their chickens cut off (see what I did there?). The left wants guns banned, period. The right does not. Everyone wants what they want but NO ONE has a logical or practical solution to advance. So, with apologies to Lewis Carroll:

"The time has come," the Walrus said,
"To talk of many things:
Of shoes--and ships--and sealing-wax--
Of cabbages--and kings--
And why the sea is boiling hot--
And whether pigs have wings."

The time has indeed come to talk of many things. Not the least of which is the society we have built for ourselves. Why is it that we have fewer guns today than we had 35 years ago, by a lot, yet the attack rate continues to climb? Is it because we have created these kill zones called "gun free" areas? Areas where every nut job who wants to take himself out of society can do so with the greatest amount of notoriety? After all, why should I blow my brains out in anonymity when I can take a bunch of folks with me at the school, church, theater, airport, etc. Take your pick. This must end

As a Vietnam veteran, I spent a lot of time around people with guns. All kinds of guns. I carried a gun for the full tour of time I was there - 365 days. There was no trigger lock, no gun safes. A .45 automatic with one in the chamber, in my shoulder holster by day, thrown over the bedpost next to my pillow each night. It was hard getting used to not having the weight of it on my shoulder when I got back, I can tell you.

So I don't fear guns as much as respect them. I remember the first time I saw someone patrolling a civilian airport with a submachine gun. It was at Schiphol in the 70's. And I remember thinking, careful with that thing, buddy, we don't need an accident here today. But that is what it has come down to. Mutually assured destruction writ small: You may kill a few of us, but you will die. A trade-off only a few are willing to make.

So, to my proposal, as distasteful as it may be to some. First, it must be understood that nut-balls are going to kill people, period, whether a total ban of guns takes place or not. So what we are talking about here is LIMITING the number of incidents, as well as the number of dead per incident. My proposal is threefold:

1. National guidelines established that identify dangerous nut-balls from, say, your aunt Tilley who just needs a little counseling from time-to-time. And, that those dangerous ones be banned from gun ownership. Further, that anyone who facilitates that person having a gun, whether purchasing on their behalf, right up through careless storage, be prosecuted as a co-defendant in whatever crimes are committed with those weapons. That ought to cut down on some of what is going on.

2. National guidelines established for armed guards at every venue that is currently thought of as gun free. Local jurisdictions can decide if they want to implement those guidelines, or not. It is suggested that in the case of schools, these be carried out by plainclothes persons and

that qualified teachers be allowed to carry concealed weapons as well.

3. Mandatory gun safety training in high schools. We can at least create a generation of citizens who understand what guns are, what they are capable of and teach them to respect not fear them. Before you go all batshit on me, they would not be working with real guns, just theoretical ones. Kinda like sex education (sorry, couldn't resist).

Okay, that is my solution, what is yours? And don't give me 'nothing changes' or 'total banning of guns'. Neither one will work and as far as I'm concerned, anyone who advances either of those solutions is just playing politics.

****

Others Titles by David Ammons:

Once Upon A Time In The 60s

Lament For The Devil

Contact the author:

dave.ammons@gmail.com

Selection of author's photo's:

davidammons.smugmug.com

Made in the USA
Las Vegas, NV
27 February 2022

44714381R00174